# *Copernicus Conundrum*

Don DeBon

**Copernicus Conundrum**

Don DeBon

First Printing
Copyright © 2022 Don DeBon

**ISBN** 978-1-948819-09-1
**ISBN** 978-1-948819-13-8**(e-book)**

All rights reserved. This publication is copyright. Apart from any fair dealing for the purpose of private study, research, criticism or review, as permitted under the Copyright Act, no part may be reproduced by any process without written permission. Inquiries should be made to the publisher. Thank you for respecting the hard work of this author.

All characters in this publication are fictitious and any resemblance to real persons, living or dead, is purely coincidental.

# Contents

# Chapter 1

Down the extended metal corridor a figure in a long brown coat, limped his way towards the transport tube. The colder temperatures increasing the staggered gate. Gabe hated going this far down in the station's depths, but the client wanted him to follow every lead. Dirt and unused and corroded components littered the edges of the hallway. Most of the doors didn't work, even if their indicators said otherwise. But most were dark, with vacant holes where their lights once sat.

Gabe kept looking over his shoulder. His Retar-428's eyes scanning for the slightest hint of motion. They were old, like the rest of him, but still working perfectly. He kept every part in pristine order. Well, except for his right leg. Damage from a blast 50 years ago, shortly after the station was finished, killed one of his servos causing a limp. He could have fixed it, but when people kept seeing him as a human with that limp, he left it. A simple modification allowed him to boost the power in the other servos and remove the limp if he had to move fast.

*In this business, the more you keep them guessing, the better off you are. Especially when you aren't human.*

Gabe took another last look around when he reached the tube and stuck his synth-skin encased hand in the slot. His eyes flashed as data raced past his vision. 'Access Granted' flashed in his vision and the tube opened. He slipped inside and slammed his palm on the close. As the door began to slide closed, bolts of light zinged through the air and stuck near his head. He dove to the side, pulling out his trusty TAC-23 out of its holster under his coat as the door continued closing. Scents of hot metal and ozone wafted over his olfactory sensors.

He saw a shadow in the back corner of the corridor, just beyond the resolving power of his optics. He tried to force them to discern the shadow, but all he got was a grainy, blurry figure. Even infrared didn't show much more. The figure was human shaped, but that could be anything these days. He aimed a stun blast and his finger started squeezing the trigger as the figure moved. Another bolt zinged towards him a half second too late and hit the door of the tube as it sealed.

Gabe let out a human-like sigh and punched the button for one of the upper levels. This job just got a whole lot more interesting.

Gabe sauntered back to his office. It wasn't on one of the top floors of the station, but it was decent up here. Unlike the lower depths. The rent was a killer, but worth it. And he usually didn't have any problems finding clients. Being the only android on Copernicus Station still around, fifty years after its construction had advantages anyone new couldn't hope for. Not to mention he had a name for getting the job done. Whatever that might be.

He also had hacked the central network and his credentials changed. As far as anyone else knew, he was human. And even scans would show the same thanks to some bio-mimetic additions he had installed at one point.

The tough part was age, he didn't quite look it. But with wrinkles added to his skin and a touch of grey added to his synth hair gave enough of an aged image, if someone didn't dig too deep. In another twenty years he would have to go somewhere else and start again or raise suspicions. But for now, Copernicus Station was still his home.

Gabe's optics went wide as he approached his office door. The full-length synth-rosewood rectangle sat ajar, and a shadow danced around inside. He boosted the power to the servos in his right leg, drew his TAC-23, and ran for the door. He dove through it, rolled along on the thick red carpet runner, and popped up with his weapon drawn in the direction of the shadow, his finger already tightening on the trigger.

A woman with long curly blonde hair, wearing a green pencil dress that stretched down to her knees, stood wide-eyed. "Gabe! Oh my gosh! You scared me to death!" Linda patted her chest as she calmed her racing heart, crossed her arms, and shifted weight from one high-heeled foot to the other. "What in the world are you doing?"

Gabe shook his head as he got to his feet and slipped his TAC back in its holster under his long coat. "Me? What are you doing leaving the door open like that? How many times have I told you never to leave the door open a crack? It is an open invitation for trouble. Not to mention you don't have the full lights on in here? What is up with that?" He looked towards the ceiling. "Lights, on full."

The recessed lighting above winked and increased to full

brightness, leaving Linda blinking fast despite the softening from the matching synth-rosewood panels that covered the walls. Her hands went to her hips as she glared at Gabe. She waved her right arm in the air while her left hand stayed on her hip. "The air reclamator system broke down again in here and I had it open a crack for circulation!"

"Again? R34 said it was fixed last time. I'm going to have his circuits for this!" Gabe silently cursed. His emotional system had erupted without its usual check. He dialed it back, and adjusted his voice back to normal.

"Hey don't be so hard on him. You know he is working day and night just trying to keep up with all the break downs lately."

Gabe inclined his head, the brim of his hat drooping down. "Yes, but I would hope something he fixed would last more than a day." He turned, slipped the duster off his shoulders, and hung it on an old-fashioned coat rack that sat to the right of the door. While most people would use a fresher system, Gabe preferred the coat rack. Not to mention, it didn't break down.

"Yeah, I know. Hey, how did you come in here like that? I didn't think your leg would let you do those kinds of moves?"

Gabe lowered the power to the servos in his leg, allowing the limp to return. He only hired Linda a couple of months ago, and even though he didn't need an assistant, it did make him look more human. "Oh that, well, I saw the door. Thought you might be in danger and adrenaline took over. I didn't even notice it. But I do now and it is going to be cranky for days."

"Awww, you were worried about me?" She walked over to him, her heels clicking loudly on the hard floor that matched the walls, and planted a kiss on his lips. "That's so sweet."

Gabe's facial systems increased their heat output in his cheeks, causing the syth-skin over them to turn a rosy red. "Yeah ... well ... I was." He had never been more happy one of the upgrades added lip heaters and blush capabilities.

She hugged him. "I never had a boss before that cared."

He looked down at the woman wrapped around his chest. "Never? I find that hard to believe."

She untangled herself and walked back towards her desk, her skirt swishing back and forth as she did. "Well, it's true. Most men are total pigs and when you told me how you wanted me to dress in here, I was worried you were one, too."

Gabe let out a chuckle. "Yes, I can imagine. But my reasons are purely to give the look of an old-fashioned office. Not to mention, it helps them feel at ease. Most in my business have some kind of robo assistant. But I prefer the real thing." He winked.

Linda smiled. "I'm happy you do. I need this job." Her smile grew. "I mean, I *really* need this job. I don't have enough credits to get back to Earth, or anywhere else."

Gabe activated the articulation servos in his face to create a large grin. "I know, and you're safe. But do not leave the door open like that again. If the air gets unbearable, call R84, leave, and lock the office. Make sure to leave a note on the door so our clients know we have an air problem. They will come back."

Linda nodded. "Sure thing, Boss."

Gabe cringed inwardly. The black-market emotion upgrades were doing their job a little too well. He hated being called 'Boss'. He started for his private office behind Linda's desk, stopped, and turned. "Any messages?"

"Oh yes! I almost forgot! Mr. Heller called again."

His eyes drifted half closed and blew out a breath from

mechanical lungs. "Again? That figures. I should have known he wouldn't wait until I finished my search like I asked."

Linda shrugged. "Yes, and he was even more, um, animated than last time."

Gabe didn't know how the man could be anymore animated. He practically yelled, then pulled the cable from the terminal instead of turning it off to cut the connection. But the man could afford a new one, unlike everyone else. "All right, I will contact him. Same location, I assume?"

Linda nodded. "Mm-hmm, and can I watch?"

Gabe let the emotion through in a small chuckle. "No, you can't watch."

"Awww please? I just want to see how an expert handles a client." She winked.

Gabe grabbed the brass knob, turned it, pulled the door to his private office open, and glanced back over his shoulder. "Surrre you do." He moved inside and shut the door before Linda could say anything more.

Gabe walked on the low pile brown carpet, moving past the well padded black couch along the wall and the chair sitting in front of the desk. The wall opposite the couch sported a small round window. He often focused his optics out the window when running multiple simulations.

Gabe moved around behind the antique real wooden desk that had cost him a small fortune. Even more for the special customizations he had installed. He pulled out the matching high-backed padded chair and sat in it. Such a comfortable chair was not something he needed, but it did make him look more human. The synth-leather squeaked at his quick decent, and he tapped a control on the squarish console that sat in the right corner of the desk. A second later, the image of Mr.

Heller's stern face in his signature white suit appeared. "I assume you have good news for me?"

"No, not yet anyway."

The man hopped up from his chair and Gabe could have sworn his red hair went three shades warmer. "You promised me results!"

"Sir, I did. But you need to give me the time I require to get those results. And keep in mind the results may not be what you hope."

Heller's eyes narrowed, and he looked about ready to jump through the screen and strangle Gabe. "I was told you are the best. And now I find out my trust is misplaced?"

"Not at all, sir. I am the best on this station. And in fact the whole quadrant, but I don't understand the impatience. You said you lost the package years ago when you were aboard last, if that be the case, and it is still here. Why the rush?"

"That is none of your business. I hired you to find it. And that is what you will do, or you will hear from my lawyers." His eyes narrowed further. "And you don't want that." Heller grabbed a cable sticking out from the side of his console and yanked. The screen dissolved into pixilated blobs as the connection cut.

Gabe leaned back in his chair and forced an articulator in his back to make a human sounding *crack*. Why would Heller be so concerned now? His body language didn't make sense regarding the situation. The item he lost almost fifty years ago on the station is unlikely still here. And his first conversation was quite calm. The added emotion didn't make sense, and each subsequent conversation showed increasing agitation. A lost present from his now-dead wife wouldn't normally cause a human to grow so agitated at the lack of its recovery.

Certainly not after fifty years. Something else was going on. But what?

Gabe leaned back towards his desk and hit a hidden button near the edge of the wooden facade. "Linda? I have a job for you."

Linda opened the door and walked into the room with her heels making loud noises even through the carpet. "What is it Boss?"

Gabe's optics narrowed. "I want you to find out when Mr. Heller was aboard the station last."

Linda blinked. "But didn't he tell you that?"

Gabe nodded in a very human fashion. "He did, but something doesn't fit. You have seen his agitation? He shouldn't be acting this way for a small memento he lost almost fifty years ago."

Linda sucked in her bottom lip. "You have a point. But do you realize it will take me hours to track this down?"

Gabe smiled. "Yes, I know the data in the station's core is fragmented going that far back. There was an accident back then and damage to the core caused a lot of data to lose its linkage."

Linda blinked. "Is that what happened? Why in the world didn't they fix it?"

Gabe lifted his right shoulder and let it drop. "I don't know, to be honest. I have asked about it many times over the years. The response was always the same: no time. However, it would have saved a lot of time. I always suspected there was more to the situation."

Linda sat down in the well-padded black chair in front of Gabe's desk. It matched his own, except for a much lower back. "Such as?"

Gabe stood up. "Such as a cover-up. Someone wanted that

data corrupted beyond reason and had enough clout to make sure no one ever tried to recover it."

"But who? And why?"

"Good questions. And neither I have been able to find answers to. See what you can dig up in the core about Mr. Heller."

"Sure thing, Boss." Linda stood and her heels gave reduced clicks on the thin carpet as she left the room.

Gabe could do this research just as well as Linda, better in fact, but he suspected someone was watching him. But doubtful they would be watching for Linda. She was too new, her access codes had only been granted last week. No one would know who she is, at least not for another week or two. Giving him time.

But time to do what is the question.

Gabe sat back down in his chair and leaned back. He had been aboard the station longer than anyone, yet even he didn't know everything about the lower depths. Originally, they were the same, nothing different at all other than being the main support areas for the station. Then at one point something . . . *happened*.

It started only one year after the station went online. Unexplained malfunctions threatened the station's operations. The Oxygen generators failed again and again even with brand-new reclamation systems. Gravity also became unstable, either increasing or decreasing. Never enough to threaten lives, but enough to wreak havoc. Power systems weren't immune either, but whatever it was occurred to a lesser degree.

At one point they had replaced almost everything on those decks yet, the problems didn't diminish. Eventually, they moved all the support systems to higher decks, sealed the lower ones, and declared them hazardous. Which kept most people from ever setting foot down there.

Still, once in a while over the years, he had to go find some fool who had bypassed the normal lockouts and ended up trapped down there. While station security sometimes listened to the pleas of whoever stayed above to go check, they never found anyone.

Gabe always had, but never alive was the problem. The bodies were often mangled beyond belief, but what did it, or how. He never found out. Someone taking pot-shots at his head today was the first real clue he had in years. He had been down there many times and had never seen anyone, let alone tried to take his head off. Something had changed, and he had a feeling Heller was the reason. Either that or it was a huge coincidence. And Gabe didn't believe in them.

He stood up and walked out of his private office. Linda sat at the console on her desk, staring at the screen. She looked up in time to see him take his duster off the rack, grab his hat, and put them on. "Going out, Boss?"

"Yes, I'm going to track down R84 and see if I can get him to fix the circulation problem in here."

She nodded. "Right Boss, and do you want me to call you when I get this done?"

Gabe let his facial articulators slip into a lopsided grin. "Sure, but don't give any details. I don't want anyone to know what we are doing, for now anyway."

Linda's head shot up. "Is there a problem with me doing this?"

"Of course not. You have the clearances. But as I said, something smells about this situation and until we know the reason, I want everything kept quiet."

Linda nodded. "Gotcha Boss."

Gabe could hear her nails tapping on the console as he slipped through the office front door and into the corridor. He checked the public console near the lift tube for R84's whereabouts. An internal image of the station showing the various decks and support systems appeared but lacked a location of the repair unit. *Very unusual, R84 always has his location linked to the central system.* He remembered the robot saying he had to install a new power cell into one of the upper suites today. He stuck his hand into the tube's access slot and hopped in as the door opened, taking off for a suite five decks up.

The tube opened to marble flooring and elegant white corridor walls. While Gabe had been up here before, he hadn't in a long time. His clients usually weren't this rich, or had any dealings with people on deck twenty-three. He stepped out onto the deck and the tube whooshed shut behind him.

Looking up and down the elegant corridor with expensive hanging golden lighting, he spotted a security guard heading towards him. *Great, he would be on patrol up here now.*

The guard wearing the usual black uniform with silver trim frowned and folded his arms. "Gabe, what are you doing up here? You know this level is restricted unless you have cleared access."

Gabe let his facial articulators form the best smile he could muster as he took two limping steps towards the man. "Murphy! So good to see you. How is your wife and kids?"

Murphy glared daggers. "Don't give me that crap. You know you aren't supposed to be up here. If you were cleared, you would show me the clearance. Either head back towards the tube or I'm taking you down to holding."

Gabe continued the smile. "Come on Murphy, our cycling

system in the office is on the friz again. I tried to get in touch with R84, but his location isn't being broadcast on the system. I knew he had an appointment up here today to install a new power cell in one of the suites. I just thought I could catch him before the air got thick enough I could cut it with an energy scalpel."

Murphy's stern expression softened. "Gotcha. Yeah, I know the cyclers are giving everyone problems lately. Okay, you can go talk with R84, but after that, you head right back down. Got it?"

Gabe nodded. "Of course. Thanks Murph, you are a saint."

Murphy waved at him. "Don't try buttering me up. It won't do you any good. Just get to R84 and get out. He's in Suite 5, third one on the left." Murphy jerked a thumb over his shoulder.

Gabe continued the smile and inclined his head. "Thanks." He took off, making sure his limp could be seen from the Murphy's position as he entered the tube. Gabe found the third door open a crack and his audio pickups detected a driver in use.

Pushing on the real wooden door, it slid open, revealing R84 half inside a wall mounting with several pieces of equipment. The robot detected the door creek as it opened and he stopped, his silver head rotating around to face the noise. His white optics flashed. "Gabe? Are you authorized to be in this section?"

Gabe allowed his optics to go straight up in an eye roll. "You too? I just had it with Murphy as well."

R84's tinny voice continued. "You know the station rules." The robot's shiny metal body extracted itself from the wall and stood up. "If you cannot produce the proper verifications, I must report you to station security."

Gabe allowed his head to fall and shake in a very human fashion. "R84, I told you just talked with Murphy, he said I could be here."

"While it is probable Station Security Agent Murphy was on this deck in the past five minutes, if he gave you such authorization, you could produce it. Therefore, I must report you to–"

Gabe held up his hands. "Now just wait a minute! He said I could find you, then I had to leave. That is why I am here."

The robot paused. "Why? You could always contact me through the station's central system."

"I could, if it was working. It didn't have your location."

The robot's optics flashed. "My location is currently off while I complete the installation of a new power core. The messaging system is still intact."

Gabe didn't want R84 to know his suspicions or have them aired on the central system. He blinked. "Is it? I figured it wouldn't work if your beacon was off."

R84 wasn't falling for it. "My memories indicate you know one is not linked to the other."

Gabe sighed. "Look, can we get past this and put my office on your priority list to have the cycler fixed?"

R84's arms dropped. "The cycler has failed again? It has not been forty-eight hours since the last repair. The odds of this happening twice are two billion-three hundred-fifty-four-thousand to one."

Gabe shrugged. "That bad? Well, all I can tell you is, it is having issues again. Would you please check it out? I have a client in a few hours."

R84's metal dome dropped. "I will investigate after my current task is complete."

Gabe turned to leave. "That is all I ask."

# Chapter 2

Gabe opened the door to his office to find Linda sitting at her desk drumming her fingers, something he learned she always did when perplexed. "Okay, what's the problem? I could hear your fingers half-way down the hall."

Linda's head popped up. "Huh? Oh, sorry Boss. Well, it's just I finished checking into Mr. Heller–"

"Oh, and the data don't track?"

Linda chewed the inside of her cheek, then let out a long sigh. "Well, it does, and it doesn't. Kinda weird."

"What do you mean? Heller isn't what he says he is?"

"No, not at all. He seems to. All the information tracks back to what he told us. But you taught me to dig deeper as there is always more beneath the surface." She tapped several keys on her console and pointed to the screen. Gabe walked around her desk and stood behind her low-backed chair to see what she was pointing at. She moved her finger along several lines of data, stopping at several spots. "And I found some data entry points were only four months old. Even though the normal date on the data is much older and matches with what he told us. And that makes little sense. Even if it was an error, it wouldn't be that quick."

She paused, folding her arms as she sat back in her chair. "Even more strange, I don't find any reference to him being aboard before. Everything else tracks, except this. At least with the station's logs. Outside logs show him here, but not the logs on the station."

Gabe let his emotion system take over. He rubbed his chin and allowed the cover over his left optic to squeeze up. "The data is damaged and fragmented. I assume you verified the checksum?"

Linda nodded. "I did, just like you taught me. He wasn't on the station. Sure, the core is a mess from that time, but that section is one of the few areas in remarkably good shape."

Gabe moved out from behind her desk, placed his hat and duster on the rack, turned, and stuck his hands into his pants pockets. "So he lied."

"Looks like it Boss. But like I said, everything else tracks. But then we have that data point abnormality, not to mention the core doesn't agree. Most people would say it can't be trusted, but I think we can in this case."

"I agree." His optics narrowed, then widened. He turned back, took his coat, hat, and put them on.

"Where are you going now?"

Gabe twisted on his heel to face Linda. "Back down to the lower depths."

Linda sat forward and blinked. "Why? You were just there."

"Because someone tried to take my head off earlier today, and I want to know why."

"What? You didn't tell me that!"

Gabe allowed the articulators in his face to crack a grin. "You didn't ask. And I didn't want to worry you."

"Gosh, no wonder you dove into the office and almost shot me!"

"I didn't almost shoot you. Yes, I did dive into–"

"Close enough!"

Gabe took two steps forward, leaned close, and let the gaze from his optics soften. "Linda, I would never shoot you."

"I would hope so," she paused to stick her tongue out, "I can just see you trying to explain that one to security."

"Yes, that would be difficult." Gabe paused a moment to allow his articulation servos to generate a mischievous grin, then turned, opened the main office door the rest of the way, and stepped through. *But I have had to explain a lot worse.*

Gabe stepped into the lift tube after slipping his hand into the access slot along the wall. This time, he went lower than before, bypassing several lockout protocols, to OD1, the first deck finished on Copernicus Station.

The tube door slid open and his optics adjusted to the dim light. No one had been down here in some time, judging by the stale air and dust on the deck plates. Gabe stepped out and the tube door whooshed shut behind him.

He stood back and activated the infrared mode in his optics.

No heat sources in sight. Still, he wasn't taking any chances and drew his TAC-23 as he stepped forward from the tube door, leaving footprints in the otherwise smooth surface of grime. His olfactory systems were awash in dust, dirt, old lubricant, and even a few molecules of aftershave. *Wait a minute. If no one has been down here so long for the dust to accumulate to this thickness, there shouldn't be any residue of a person's aftershave. Those molecules break down in a few days, not years.*

Gabe scanned the area more closely. Activating several enhancements brought up areas where the dirt was disturbed, then carefully altered to appear unchanged.

*That is a lot of effort to go though, not to mention I am not sure how it could even be done to this level.*

His optics flashed as he peeled back the layers, revealing trace outlines of human footprints leading away from the tube and down the aisles of what they left of the original station support systems. He allowed his vision to narrow as he took several careful steps. While he didn't see any signs of entrapment, he wasn't about to take a chance, either.

This level had more junk than anything else. Everything from used oxygen generators to dead power system were left either in piles along the walls or where they were pulled. Due to this deck's service-only nature, enclosing walls were rarely used, leaving the different components open and visible unlike other levels. Twisted pipes, some rusted, stretched out, separating each section. Normally, they would have been replaced, but no one came down here.

Except someone did, and recently. Then covered their tracks in a way Gabe couldn't determine how.

He moved between the twisting pipes and dilapidated equipment with deliberate slowness. He couldn't detect any movement or heat signatures. The level was stone-cold dead. Yet someone had taken the time to erase any trace they were here. *Why?*

He navigated the maze of broken, ramshackle equipment, but when he passed an old water reclamation unit, he stopped. His optics flagged several sections that had a slight increase in light reflection. He zoomed in. Sure enough, someone had taken this whole unit apart and carefully put it back together. However, each connection point showed a slight change, but only to his enhanced optics. No one else would have noticed.

Again he wondered, *why*? It was one thing to cover your tracks to hide you were ever here. Even if he didn't know how they did it, it could be they didn't want the possibility of a call from station security. Gabe let his facial articulators crack a grin. *Not that they have cared about these levels in decades.* But to take apart old, useless, broken equipment, and then reassemble it? This took the mystery to a whole new level.

Gabe carefully scanned the reclamator and removed a pipe from the central section and peered in. Activating the infrared in his optics, he saw the central filter, but someone had cut large sections from it. It almost looked like old Earth Swiss cheese after a mouse had chewed on it.

He pulled his head from the hole and replaced the pipe. Not only did this person disassemble the entire unit, but carved sections from the central filter. The filters had zero recovery value, which is why they had been left here as junk. Easier to leave than to remove. But whoever it was only carved out sections. Why not take the entire filter?

Gabe continued on the meandering path between rusted pipes and derelict equipment. Eventually, he came across another oddity. A carbon dioxide scrubber had faint signs of being reassembled. He twisted one of the connectors and popped it open. The inside looked similar to the reclamator, with sections missing from the sodium hydroxide core.

Someone had to be looking for something. But what? And whatever it is, must have been on the station for a long time, or they wouldn't bother looking on this deck.

Behind the scrubbers, he found other environmental systems also carefully disassembled, their cores dissected and reassembled.

He knew Mr. Heller was more than he appeared, and this proved it. It was unlikely he was behind this, but the probability was high he was after the same thing. Whatever *that* was.

He needed more information, and for that, he needed to do a deep dive into the station's core. While he could do it from here, if he got one of the access panels to work. But, if someone was watching, it would raise a lot of warning bells. His office system had special equipment to hide his connection, should it be necessary. And now it was.

Gabe turned round and headed back towards the lift.

# Chapter 3

Gabe stepped out of the lift and walked down the hallway with his usual limp, stopping at the door to his office. It was closed and sealed this time, as it should be. He placed his hand on the access panel and it lit up green, causing the hidden bolts around the door to click as they retracted. He pushed open the door. The air smelled fresh.

Linda looked up from the console on her desk. "Gabe! You just missed R84! He fixed our air cycler!" She paused to take a deep breath. "It's so much better."

Gabe activated his facial articulators, creating a wide grin. "I can tell. I saw him earlier and persuaded him to come down here to take a look after he was finished with his current project."

Linda blinked. "That fast? What did you do? Bribe him with a fresh can of oil?"

Gabe's grin grew. "Well, I might have mentioned I had a client coming today."

Linda blinked again as her head shot back and her body straightened. "We do?"

"No, but don't tell R84."

Linda winked as she relaxed. "It will be our secret."

Gabe pulled off his hat and coat, sticking them on the rack, and took two steps towards his private office. He stopped. "Anything else?"

Linda shook her head. "Nope. I tried to dig further into the old station records to see if I missed Mr. Heller the first time, but ran into a stream of corrupted data. If he was here, I bet is in that mess. Want me to try again?"

Gabe activated the articulators in his shoulders, allowing his head to shake back and forth. "No, no need. I will see what I can dig up. If anyone comes looking for me, I'm not here. Got it?"

Linda nodded. "Right, Boss."

Gabe took several more steps, tapped a control to the right of the synth-wood door to his office, stepped through, and the door slid shut behind him. He moved around behind his desk and sat in the black high-backed synth-leather chair. He linked to the console on it, and closed his visual receptors.

Data flooded in from the core as he wrangled for control and activated every stealth system he had. It was possible someone could spot his entrance, if they were looking at the right moment, but it would be slight. And they would have to know what to look for. His signature wasn't that of a normal human or even an android. Though, it might raise someone's curiosity enough to start trying a trace. And if that happened, he would have to work fast before they could complete it.

He stood on a vast three-dimensional flat plane and as he looked around, buildings began raising up around him. After a few moments, an immense city built itself around him, and he started walking from building to building. Data zinged back and forth around him on beams of light. He continued on, progressing deeper and deeper into the core. And as he did, the buildings changed, looking older and some of them dark or had damaged walls with gaping fissures running throughout. A few were to the point of almost crumbling, and he wondered what still kept the data from degrading further. But then again, no one even knew what caused the damage in the first place.

He scanned the area, but the data was so badly fragmented he couldn't get a reliable read unless he was right on top of it. He entered one of the damaged buildings. At one point it must have been bright blue with gleaming surfaces, but now the color had turned much darker, with dirt covering everything making it look light brown. The main central cavernous area held multiple data towers jutting up from the floor. He approached the absolute center and the largest data point. The fragmentation was evident long before he even entered the area. Cracks radiated throughout, twisting, turning in on themselves and taking the data with it.

Of course, in reality it was nothing like this. But Gabe's three-dimensional interface generated the images in an attempt to untangle the intertwining data. Usually it helped. Gabe wasn't sure if it would this time. He had never been this deep inside the fragmented zone. He also shouldn't have been able to smell anything in the simulation but yet his olfactory system detected rotting decay.

Gabe touched the floor at the absolute center of the building and accessed the layer along the top. Then another, several layers below. Neither held anything of value. A few early station repair logs, even before the trouble began. And few textual communications. Nothing indicating Mr. Heller was ever here. Or what happened later on.

Though he didn't expect it to. Many people had tried to find out what happened at Copernicus Station one year after it went online. Gabe tried another level. The fragmentation increased and made access more difficult. Gabe had to flip between several points of the core to even come close to an accurate read.

Gabe's vision narrowed as he zeroed in on a different point, just three months past the other. A video communication this time. But it could not be played due to the damage. Gabe waved a hand, and a table appeared filled with different tools. He grabbed two different ones, one for repairing the file size, and the other for separating data layers.

Slicing his way in, he removed the unplayable parts and, after the checksum had been repaired, he activated the file.

A screen materialized in front of him. At first, all Gabe saw was static. Then the broken white and black dots resolved into the face of a short, fat, purple skinned entity with six arms known as the Karlan. One of the first extra terrestrials humans had encountered. While Gabe was proud of his repair of the file, it still didn't cover anything he didn't already know.

This particular Karlan was the last ship to dock at Copernicus Station before whatever happened . . . happened.

Gabe waved another hand, and the screen vanished along with the table. He tried another, deeper section. This area wasn't quite as damaged as the others. Peering in and touching the center of the building, he found the data he was looking for! Travel logs at roughly the time Mr. Heller said he was aboard.

While they didn't have as much degradation, they also refused his access. He could see the file and the date, but nothing more. Gabe allowed an audible sigh to cross his lips a few seconds before he brought out his tools again. He tried every-single-one yet it refused even the most basic access. He could get the serial number and checksum, but that was all.

And this from a file three times the size of most. While it could have been nothing more than a hollow promise. Gabe had seen too many of those. This one had data. But getting to it, without damage, and not leaving a visible trail was the trick.

This time, he accessed the data directly, not bothering to use the visual system. He ran several diagnostics and everyone said the data was intact. Yet it refused to allow him to even peer past the corner of the curtain, much less even enter.

When he ran another program that peeled away layers of data, for a moment he saw a different checksum date code before it evaporated. *Someone has been in here before and does not want anyone else to do the same. Whoever it is hasn't been here long. A few weeks perhaps, which fits in with the disassembled equipment on OD1. The faint lines in the threads would have disappeared in a month or two.*

Gabe tried several methods to try to crack into this area, but to no avail. Bruit-forcing it might damage the core further here, and station security would likely see it. Tracking it back to him would be near impossible, but still not zero.

He waved a hand and the surrounding area morphed as newer, intact buildings rose up where the dilapidated ones stood a moment before. He nodded and allowed his facial articulators to crack a grin, even though no one could see it. Walking into the nearest building, he accessed its central database. Lists of arrival codes flooded past his visual receptors. In a few seconds, he knew the names of everyone that had left or came aboard Copernicus Station in the past three months.

Nothing.

Nothing out of the ordinary at all. While he knew most of these arrivals already, he expected to have missed someone.

But no, everyone was accounted for and every-single-one had either been here before or was well known. Not one anomalous person had come aboard. He even checked the maintenance EVA airlock logs, thinking one of them might have been an ingress point, but no. They hadn't been used at all in the past three months.

Not only had this mystery person managed to use an impossible technology to hide his footprints in the lower decks, he shouldn't be here in the first place.

Gabe let out another human sigh as he severed his link and the world around him resolved once again into his office. In retrospect, he wondered why he thought someone capable of doing what he thought was impossible would come aboard in a normal fashion. Still, until now, he always thought every entrance or exit would be logged. The station was a closed system after all. No way on or off without going through an airlock. Anything else would compromise the entire hull. Yet, someone had done it. The mere thought of it caused his emotion system to send a very human shiver down his back.

Gabe leaned back in his chair as his visual receptors narrowed. And from what he could tell, they had arrived after Mr. Heller contacted him. That was too much of a coincidence to ignore. Not to mention he and Linda couldn't find any trace of Mr. Heller being aboard before. Granted, the core is in bad shape for that time period, but other things he mentioned didn't add up either.

The com in his desk buzzed as he was about to link back to the core again. "Gabe?"

Gabe let out another sigh as he tapped a hidden button the surface of his desk. "Yes, Linda?"

Her voice came through a hidden speaker in the desk. "I know you told me not to bother you, but there is a gentleman out here that is insistent on seeing you."

Gabe's optics narrowed as his articulation system cocked his head. "Don't tell me Mr. Heller is here?"

"No, it isn't him."

"Then who is it?"

"I don't know. He won't give me his name."

Gabe sat forward in his chair. This was highly unusual. None of his clients ever failed to introduce themselves. Everyone knew he wouldn't take a case if a client tried to remain anonymous. He didn't deal with *those* kinds of cases. "What?"

"I know. I even told him you wouldn't take a case unless he told me who he is and want he wants. Didn't make any difference. He just said, 'He will see me, if not now then later.' Do you want me to tell him to 'get lost'? I think is the old phrase you said people used to use?"

Gabe let his emotion system seep in for a minute, and he chuckled. "Yes, that is the phrase. Yes, tell him to 'get lost'. I will not waste my time with him."

"Okay, I did, and he just left. But he told me to mention he knows about the fresh pipe threads in the lower depths, and to look him up when you want to know more."

That piqued Gabe's interest. He had told no one about that yet, not even Linda. He stood up and dashed for the door, yanked it open, to Linda's wide eyes as he darted through, opened the outer office door, and dashed out into the corridor.

Nothing.

Gabe looked up and down the corridor. No one in sight, and no human could have moved that fast. Yet this guy had. The offices here on this level were all closed today except his, and the tube sat motionless at the end of the hall.

Gabe's head dropped as he turned around and went back

inside his office. Linda sat with her arms folded. "You want to tell me what that was all about?"

"What access code did the man give?"

Linda blinked. "Access code?"

Gabe shook his head. "Sorry, number to call. I've got a lot of things on my mind at the moment."

"I'm sure. But no, he didn't give a forwarding contact number or frequency."

Gabe's visual receptors blinked as he cocked his head. "Why didn't you get one?"

Linda's arms tightened. "He said you knew him and already had it. I didn't know I should interrogate him. What's going on?"

"No, you did the right thing. I will catch up with him later. Could you describe him?" Right now, Gabe mentally cursed himself in ten different ways he didn't get the fly-eye fixed in the outer office when it burned out two months ago.

"About your height, slim, had on an old-fashioned sport coat, I think they were called, and black pants. Brown hair and green eyes. Sorry, I wasn't paying that much attention. Shouldn't the fly-eye have an image of him?"

Gabe's facial articulation servos shoved his tongue into his cheek. "I didn't get it repaired yet."

Linda stood up and put her hands on her hips. "Well, why not! I told you weeks ago I noticed it wasn't working."

"They are expensive, R84 is very busy, and up until now, we haven't ever needed an image from it."

Linda glared. "Which is about right. You never need it until it isn't there. Which is what I said when I found it was broken."

Gabe sucked in a breath into his mechanical lungs and let it out slowly. "Yes, you are right. I should have, and I will have another talk with R84 today to have it replaced." He took several steps towards his private office as the door behind him finished closing.

Linda cocked her head. "Boss? Aren't you going to talk with that guy?"

Gabe's head turned. "Not at the moment."

"Why not? I told you what he looks like. And I doubt there are many on board dressed like that."

"Yes, I know. But when I went out in the corridor, he was already long gone."

Linda blinked. "That quick? What did he do? Run for the lift?"

"No. At least I don't think so. The lift was not engaged at all, hence I am uncertain where he went. But I suspect he will return in short order."

Linda sat back in her chair and folded her arms again. "And what makes you say that?"

Gabe allowed his articulation servos to crack a large grin. "Call it a hunch. If he shows up, show him right in. Otherwise, I am not here." He opened the door to his private office, stepped inside, and the door slid closed behind him and locked with an audible click.

Gabe sat down behind the antique desk. Well, this was an interesting development. His optics narrowed. *How did he find me? I didn't see anyone in the lower depths, yet he knew to come here with the knowledge of what I had seen?* He leaned back in his chair. *My link? Could he have traced it back to this office?*

Gabe shook his head. *No, not possible. I used too many cloaking protocols. But still . . . Well one way to find out.*

Gabe closed his optics and activated the link. The world flashed and built up around him again at the exact same point where he left.

"Okay whoever you are, time to come out and play." He leaned forward and waved an arm. High end equipment resolved in front of him. He picked up the high resolution scanner and waved it around.

Nothing.

Not a thing detected in this area of the core, and even for several sections around him were unoccupied. If the man had found him here, he didn't stick around.

Yet every one Gabe's intuitive systems said he was being watched. A thought raced through his circuits, and he almost slapped his head in a very human gesture. *Of course, he can evade my scans. Anyone capable of hiding his footprints like he did might also have the technology to cloak themselves from all kinds of scans.* "I know you are here. Show yourself!"

"You are smarter than we gave you credit for," a voice called.

"All right, shall we drop the pretext and you tell me what you want?"

"Who says I want anything?" the voice echoed.

"Are you trying to insult my intelligence further? You obviously want something. Something very important. Something others also want, and you think it is on this station. So why don't we stop dancing around each other playing this game?"

"Oh, but I thought you wanted to play?"

Right then, he wished he had chosen his words a bit better. "That was an expression, as you are no doubt aware."

"I am indeed aware. However, it is still unique to hear such expressions from an android."

Gabe's visage went blank. The man knew. But how? "Who are you?"

"No one of consequence."

"If you will excuse the old expression, *bull*. Who are you? And how do you know what I really am?"

Gabe *felt* a smile and heard a chuckle. "Very well, I will tell you this much. Your secret is safe for a long time to come. You need not worry about I, or anyone else divulging it."

Gabe allowed the image of his face to scrunch up. "That is hardly comforting, as you no doubt can imagine. I have little reason to trust you." *If I can keep him talking a little longer, I will know his exact location and be able to act.*

"You are quite correct. You have no reason to trust me. Yet you should."

Gabe looked around again and ran another scan from a device in his hand, but still couldn't locate anyone. The voice seemed to come from everywhere and nowhere at the same time. "Then you can see we are at an impasse. I should not stay here any longer, as I find it useless to debate the subject."

"Wait! As I said, you should trust me. And you must realize I have information no one else does. Doesn't that raise your curiosity?"

"It does. However, I do not see any reason to continue this, considering nothing can come from it."

"Are you so sure of that?"

In Gabe's mind, an image formed with a location and a prompt if he wished to proceed. *Gotcha.* "I am now. Thank you."

"What?"

Gabe activated a special link security protocol he had created and installed many years ago, but never used. The system lashed out full force, targeting the other end of the conversation.

Outside the office, Linda heard a shriek.

# Chapter 4

Gabe severed the link in time to see Linda rush into his private office. "I just heard something horrible just outside the door!" She stood pointing back towards the main office, waving a finger towards the outer door.

Gabe cracked a grin wider than usual, realizing she had used the emergency access override code he gave her to open the door to his private office. *At least she remembered it. I told her she couldn't write it down.* "I can imagine. Did you go out and look?"

"No! I'm not going out there! I'm a secretary, not your bodyguard!"

Gabe allowed a reverberating chuckle to escape his lips. "I wasn't *asking* you to. I wanted to make sure you didn't. That's all. Yes, you are my secretary, not a bodyguard, and I wouldn't want it any other way. Don't worry, I will take care of it." He stood up from behind the desk and walked past a wide-but-quickly-narrowing eyed Linda.

He pulled open the door and two meters from it, a man with brown hair in an old-fashioned sport jacket with black pants lay on the deck unconscious near an access terminal not three meters from his office door. The squarish recessed terminal sat darkened with clear signs of an overload, the wall now sporting a black stain on the otherwise white antiseptic corridor. The smell of burnt plastics and fried wiring wafted past Gabe's olfactory system.

Gabe moved out into the corridor, grabbed the man under his armpits, dragged him into the outer office, and through the door into his private office, leaving marks through the carpet from the man's cheap shoes. He could have carried him with ease, but didn't want to raise Linda's suspicions any further.

"Boss? What happened to him?"

Gabe shrugged as he hoisted the man's torso up onto the black couch sitting along the far wall, then rotated and slid the rest of his body up, causing a rustling of the upholstered furniture's fabric. "I have no idea."

Linda's one eye narrowed as she crossed her arms, and her foot began tapping rhythmically. "Why don't I believe you?"

Gabe shrugged, looking at the man. He fought the urge to search him. While the man could be a threat, the odds were low. Not one of his simulations pointed the man out as dangerous. A potential problem, yes, but not an outright threat.

While he knew the man was still on the station, perhaps even close by. But when his system had located him almost outside his door, he had to fight his emotion systems not to reveal outright shock.

*Right outside my door! How is that possible?* Of course, the answer was simple: a cloaking system. A powerful, very advanced, and portable cloaking system no one ever heard of. It was no wonder he didn't see the lift moving when he went after him. *He was still there!*

Gabe's emotional systems wanted to shake the man awake

and demand answers, and he even agreed. But he was certain Linda wouldn't approve.  At least not without explaining why. Something he did not want to do.

Linda turned and headed for the outer office. "I'll call for a doctor or MedMech."

Gabe raised his arm to block her exit. "No. He will be fine."

Linda's gaze turned icy, and she folded her arms. "He sure don't look fine.  Now you can move that arm or I'm calling security instead and you can find yourself a new secretary!"

Gabe dropped his arm. "Sorry. You can if you like, but he will be fine."

"Humph! He needs help!"

The man on the couch stirred as his head bobbed back and forth. "Ugh! What hit me?"  His eyes remained closed, but his hand reached up to rub his forehead. "My head feels like a planet, one that is about to explode."

Gabe allowed his articulators to crack a grin. "See? What did I tell you? He's fine."

Linda's eyes narrowed further. "He sure don't sound it."

Gabe let out a limited sigh.  "Fine, then go find a MedMech."

Linda's eyes went wide. "But you just said–"

"Never mind what I said. Go get one."

Linda eyed him, but after several seconds gave a short nod and left the office.

Gabe turned towards the man. "Now, since she is gone, are you going to tell me what you were holding back? Or do we have to go through this again?"

The man's eyes shot open.  "No, that won't be necessary. My name is Arkinon–"

Gabe's optics narrowed. "And you are from the future."

Arkinon shot up and twisted on the couch to face Gabe. "What? How?" His gaze drifted back down as a wave of dizzyness hit him and he held his head.

Gabe allowed his articulators to crack a grin. "The probability became high when I found you outside my office door moments after I had scanned the area. Not to mention you knowing my true nature. Also, your vocal patterns suggested you considered it old news and of no real consequence. Someone from the future might feel that way."

Arkinon tried to stand but fell backwards onto the couch instead. "Or they didn't feel the information was worth anything."

Gabe gave a nod. "Another possibility, however, considering I know many people that would love to use such information against me, it is unlikely."

Arkinon lowered his head. "Well played, sir. I have never been bested until now. And would you tell me what you did? You shouldn't have been able to locate me, let alone incapacitate me."

Gabe's stance stiffened, and he crossed his arms, looking down at the man. "Give me one good reason to give you any advantage?"

Arkinon smiled. "I won't tell your secretary what you really are. Or anyone else for that matter."

Gabe's optics narrowed. "If you wanted to do that, you would have earlier. Besides, that would alter your history a great deal. Something you cannot afford."

Arkinon nodded again. "Again, well played. Our records do not do you justice."

"And who is that?"

"Those from my time, approximately three hundred years from now."

Gabe offered a stone glare. "You know exactly when. I don't deal in approximations. I thought we were done playing games?"

Arkinon moved again, and this time managed to stand up. "We are. I didn't think the exact time was important. Very well, three hundred twenty-three years from now. Better?"

Gabe let out a grin that could swallow a horse. "Much better. Now, why are you here?"

Arkinon let out a brief sigh. "I know you noticed the searched equipment on OD1."

"Yes, and dust footprints that had been carefully erased by a unknown technology."

Arkinon blinked. "You saw them? How? I know the change in the threads were a possible as I couldn't remove them completely. But I didn't think anyone would notice fresh marks in old disused equipment compared to footprints."

"I have my methods. Now the question: why?"

"I have my reasons."

Gabe allowed a bit of his emotion system to seep though losing patience. "Which *are?*"

Arkinon shifted from one foot to the other. "I suppose I should tell you, and you might even be able to help me. You have already demonstrated more abilities than I would have imagined."

Gabe folded his arms again. "*And?*"

Arkinon blew out a breath. "I'm looking for something."

"That much is obvious. And I am going to assume you were the one that shot at me."

Arkinon's head dropped in a shallow nod. "Yes."

In a blur of motion, Gabe pulled out his TAC-23 from its

holster and pointed at Arkinon's head. "Now give me one good reason I shouldn't return the favor?"

"I'm from the future, and I need to recover a device that is from my time before it causes cataclysmic damage."

Gabe lowered the weapon and holstered it. "Believe it or not, I suspected you weren't from this time moments after I saw the traces on OD1. While all my simulations were against, it I couldn't imagine hiding your footprints as you did otherwise. Let alone cloaking yourself to keep me from seeing you in the corridor. I have no doubt you saw me race out of the office looking for you and watched me return."

Arkinon nodded again. "Very astute of you. Yes, I was."

"What is it you are looking for?"

Arkinon sat back down on the well-padded couch, this time for comfort rather than necessity. "It is a prototype cloaking system."

Gabe allowed his articulation servos to cock his head. "Prototype? What makes this one special? I have seen you use a fully functional cloaking system."

Arkinon sat back. "Yes I do, however, this particular unit is much more powerful and can even phase matter as part of the cloak."

Gabe's optics blinked. "Phase matter? As in allowing one object to pass through another?"

Arkinon nodded. "Correct. It is designed to be installed on star ships, as the power requirements make it impossible otherwise."

Gabe straightened. "I would call that a benefit. I would hate to think of a phasing cloak that a person could wear. The abuse of such a device would be beyond comprehension."

"Quite true. The same exists for such a ship system, although less."

"So what went wrong? An accident?"

"Very insightful of you.  Yes, there was an overload.  The inventor received several warnings of his funding being cut off.  He was trying to finish the project before it was ready. Someone rushed in, trying to stop him, warning the device was too unstable. He tried to destroy it by boosting the power systems ..."

# Chapter 5

Arkinon sat hunched over his console, looking past the screen in front of him at the several-meters-wide glass and metal booth beyond. Inside, a small cube glowed.

"More power, Miss Prandra."

Seated several meters to his right in a white lab coat with pink trim and matching shoes, a young woman's eyes went wide. "But sir, we are already twenty percent higher than we have ever used before. Shouldn't we check everything first?"

Arkinon nodded. "Yes, while I agree that would be prudent, we do not have the time. This project has been canceled and labeled a security risk. If I cannot demonstrate a fully functional prototype in forty-eight hours, we lose everything." He straightened and stuck his hands into the deep pockets on either side of his plain white lab coat.

The woman blanched. "They can't do that! We are full citizens of the–"

Arkinon sighed as he shoved his tongue into his cheek and rolled it around for several seconds. "Trust me, they can and will. Even though I don't produce a working prototype, they will confiscate everything to make sure no one else ever does either."

"But that must mean they believe it is possible and you are close?"

Arkinon shook his head. "No, more like cautious. They do not take any chances with security. Please increase the available power."

She nodded and turned several dials on her console. Inside the metal and glass cage set in a pit in the middle of the lab, the cube grew brighter as a single arc of raw energy flashed out. At that very second, the cube seemed to grow transparent.

"That is doing it!" Arkinon shouted.

Just then, a man burst into the lab wearing a dark business suit and waving a stack of papers several inches thick in his right hand. "Stop these fool experiments right now!"

"Mr. Stross! But we are so–"

Mr Stross' eyes blazed. "I don't care. These experiments are too dangerous. Stop right this instant!"

"But we have taken every precaution as you can no doubt see." Arkinon paused to move his hand in a wide sweeping gesture across the lab, stopping to point at the center with its the glass and metal booth. The consoles sat in a half-moon shape surrounding it, giving an equal view of the cage from each one.

Stross tossed the stack of paper onto the nearest console and folded his arms. "Yes, you have. Every precaution you *know* about. But there are too many variables on this project. It is simply impossible to plan for them all."

Arkinon picked up the stack and frowned, reading the top page before throwing it back down. "You were the one that got my funding cut and the security gag ordered on the project."

Stross nodded. "I was. And with good reason. Now stop these hellish experiments!"

"I won't, not when we are so close."

"Then I shall take action!" He took several quick steps and reached an empty console to Arkinon's right.

His hand went for a control, and Arkinon dove for him. But before Stross could touch anything on the panel, Prandra gasped, "Doctor Arkinon! The cube!"

Their attention immediately shot towards the glass and metal booth at the dead center of the room. Inside, the cube's glow radiated out in a blinding white light far above anything they had seen before.

"Shut it down! Lower the power like I showed you and initiate the emergency shut down protocol to the system," Arkinon said.

"I have! It refuses giving a life warning error!"

Arkinon winced. The system could deny such a command, but only if the station had cloaked and terminating the system now might cause the loss of hull integrity.

Stross waved his arms. "Now, do you see these experiments are too dangerous? Your poor judgment is going to kill us all!"

Arkinon ignored the man. "Terminate all power! Now!"

Miss Prandra blinked. "But!"

"Override all the safeties!" Arkinon jammed his palm on a reader next to the console in front of him. "Arkinon 7576omega-alpha-gamma-457 override all power systems aboard and shut down."

"Access approved Doctor Arkinon," a soft calm voice came over speakers imbedded in the ceiling. "Override acknowledged. Shutting down all power systems aboard."

Every light in the room went dark except for the control

consoles and two emergency lights in the corners, giving them enough light to see. Arkinon looked up to the glass and metal cage to see the cube growing even brighter. The man next to Arkinon pointed towards the cage. "Why is it still doing that? Didn't you deactivate all power sources?"

"Yes, I did. But because you distracted me, it has reached a point of not needing it!"

Stross blanched. "I distracted? If you recall, I came in to stop this experiment, nothing more."

Arkinon turned to face the man. "Yes you! If you hadn't interfered, we wouldn't be having this problem."

The man blinked. "I interfered? So now I went from a distraction to outright interference?" He paused to jab his finger in Arkinon's face. "Don't try to pin this on me. You are the one that is to blame, not me."

"Doctor! The device!" Miss Prandra had stood up, pointing towards the containment area.

Arkinon turned in time to see the cube glowing even brighter and sending flashing out arcs of energy lighting up the entire room. They all began to feel a sudden dizziness as the world shifted for a microsecond and returned.

Arkinon's eyes went wide as his hands danced across the controls in front of him. "It isn't accepting any of my commands and is continuing to build power."

Stross' eyes went wide as his head jutted back. "How is that possible? You terminated all power-generating systems aboard, didn't you?"

Arkinon nodded. "I did. But the device is capable of pulling power directly from the core's potential output. It doesn't need to be engaged."

"Are you insane? Why would you give a device such a capability?"

Arkinon turned. "It was something the military wanted. I didn't want to add it, but they threatened to terminate my funding unless I included the feature. Their theory was, if it could pull power from an enemy, why not? Save our own reserves while depleting theirs. In the end, I had to agree, wireless power transfer had advantages."

The device in the containment area flashed again, and the world shifted as it grew even brighter. "What is that?"

Arkinon sighed. "You don't want to know."

Stross grabbed Arkinon by the lapels of his white lab coat and shook him. "Yes I do!"

"The device is trying to phase the entire facility."

Stross blinked and took a step back. "Phase? You mean you actually did it? Created a phasing cloak? You *are* insane. It will cause a destabilization of the entire facility!"

Arkinon smiled. "Normally yes, with prolonged exposure. But I found a way to do it safely."

A white-hot arc of lightning flashed inside the glass and steel cage, causing all of them to shield their eyes as the world shifted again. "It's getting worse!"

Arkinon sighed, his fingers flying over his console. "I know. It should stop soon. With each such burst, its reserves are diminished. While it could potentially pull more, it won't now that it is trying to phase."

Stross pointed towards the cage. "And what happens if it manages to partially phase this facility and not return it to full solidarity?"

Arkinon shook his head. "Not possible. I have built in too many safeguards."

"But if it fails midway, it could!"

"Again, not possible. It is only running tests now to see

what it can and can't do before attempting a full phase. It will determine it can't, and will shut down."

"So you say! I would rather have it work fully than half-way!" Stross pushed Arkinon out of the way, and he fell to the floor. Stross jammed a control on the console all the way up. Stored emergency power from the console itself flowed into the device.

Arkinon picked himself off of the floor and dove back towards the console. *"Nooo."* He punched Stross in the shoulder, pushing him back, and pulled the control back down. It was too late. The cube in the cage flashed white, then red as the surrounding glow grew even brighter. Arcs of white power erupted out, filling the cage in a deadly display as the center of the cube flashed, expanding out in a bright bubble of blue-white energy, and disappeared.

# Chapter 6

Gabe's stood in front of Arkinon leaning forward, his optics went wide. "Seems as though boosting power like that would be even more dangerous than letting it subside."

Sitting on the sofa, Arkinon nodded as his fingers laced together in his lap. "It was. The energy backlash ruptured the space-time continuum, engulfed the device, and sent it back in time. I didn't know when and I have been searching ever since."

Gabe took several steps over to his desk, then turned back. "And I am going to assume you don't normally have time-travel. How did you search?"

A grin spread across Arkinon's face and he nodded, leaning back. "You are correct, we didn't. An analysis of the data allowed me to recreate the anomaly that engulfed the device, but with more control. I also made a portable system to allow me to return without needing to leave the crack open. Removing the possibility of it closing prematurely and leaving me stranded in a different time."

Gabe's optics narrowed. "You are the inventor of this device, aren't you? The same Arkinon?"

Arkinon nodded again. "Yes, and I must recover it. Part

of my data was destroyed when it time-jumped, and I can't rebuild it without the copy of the schematics stored in its core. Not to mention there is another problem that I didn't realize until recently. And is how I found out it must be on this station."

"Which is?"

"Its power systems are incompatible with the systems from this time. It can cause damage or fluctuations to any system nearby."

Gabe leaned up against his desk. "And how big is it? What exactly does it look like?"

Arkinon sighed, raising his right hand with his index finger and thumb spread apart two inches. "About this big. It is a small black cube that can fit in your hand. The sides are covered in a nondescript pattern, and of course it can glow depending on if activated or not."

Gabe's optics flared. "That small? I thought you said it could only work aboard ships?"

"Due to the power levels required, yes."

Gabe stared at the man. He knew he was holding back but not sure what as complex formulas flashed through his optics. "It seems to me if you were able to determine the device slipped into the past, you should be able to track where and when."

Arkinon moved forward to the edge of the couch, causing the fabric to rustle. "You would think so, and at one point, I did as well. However, tracking it proved impossible due to the nature of the instability. I tried multiple times but couldn't find it. Then I realized it must have moved through space as well as time. It could be anywhere."

Gabe folded his arms as his optics narrowed. "Then how did you know it was here?"

"I didn't at first. Later on, I realized if it was still activated it might draw upon any nearby power source. And considering they are incompatible in this time, it could show up as undetermined power and equipment failures."

Gabe nodded. "I see. And which might explain all the early issues with this station."

Arkinon bobbed his head up and down. "Yes, exactly."

"If this is true, why didn't you arrive then instead of now?"

"I tried. Every attempt resulted in an unstable time rift. It would have killed me to step through. This is as close as I could get."

Gabe pushed himself off of the desk, still keeping his arms folded. "And why is that?"

Arkinon shook his head and gave a shrug. "I really don't know. It might be the device has exhausted all sources of power it can tap into and being partially powered before by the available sources in this time prevented me from jumping any closer."

Gabe cocked his head as he leaned closer. "But you said they are incompatible."

"They are, but it is theoretically possible it could still access them on some level."

Gabe straightened as his gazed drifted off of Arkinon and onto the nearby window as further simulations flashed through his optics. "Hmm. Everything has been moved from the original decks for years now. Perhaps it did finally run out of power."

Arkinon nodded. "Yes, I feel that is the most probable reason."

"I would assume you didn't find it yet or you wouldn't have tried to take my head off earlier."

Arkinon winced. "I would not have injured you. At the time, I assumed you were searching for the device as well."

Gabe's optics narrowed. "I beg to differ. Those blasts were too close to be warning shots."

Arkinon shook his head. "No, I am able to place even closer shots without issue. My equipment is very precise."

*I don't know what he is trying to pull, but his heart rate keeps spiking. He is outright lying or hiding something.* Gabe nodded. "That is good to hear. I must admit the situation had me wondering."

The front office door opened and Linda stepped through with a MedMech right behind her.

"The injured man is right in here," Linda said, ushering the Mech into the office and moving past her desk to Gabe's private office.

But when she entered, all was not as she expected.

The cylindrical Mech rotated on his anti-grav cushion, scanning the area as several arms extended, each ending in a medical device. It floated into Gabe's private office and stopped.

"I do not detect anyone in distress. Please state the nature of the medical emergency."

Linda saw the man sitting on the couch still wearing the same sports jacket, although she noticed several points on the cuffs appeared singed that weren't there before. He stood and smiled. "I don't know what you are talking about. Everyone is fine here," the man said.

Linda put her hands on her hips and glared at Gabe as her high-heeled foot began tapping. "Well?" Gabe raised his right shoulder while lowering his left in a half-hearted shrug. She turned to face the MedMech. "I'm sorry. Apparently, I overreacted to the situation."

The floating Mech turned left and right twice, scanning the room again before focusing on Linda. "While we are always pleased when a patient recovers and no longer requires our services, to give false information about a patient is in dire need of our services, when they are not, is grounds for penalty regarding statute 342 of the station code." It paused to turn and scan again before continuing. "However, I understand this is a case of simple misunderstanding and no penalty will be logged against you. But please do keep this in mind for the future." The Mech turned and floated out of the room.

Linda whirled around to face Gabe. "That is the *last* time I go looking for a MechMech! *You* can do it from now on!"

Gabe cracked a grin and suppressed a chuckle. "They won't penalize you even if you did it again. You would have to do it many times before security would get involved."

Linda took three quick steps and stuck her finger in his face. "That is not the point! I don't want a black mark on my record here. It might cause problems when I go somewhere else."

Gabe shook his head. "I can't imagine that. They won't make any changes to your records unless a formal complaint is logged, and that requires security getting involved."

"So you say!" Linda humphed. She turned away for several seconds to let the heat fade from her face before she turned back and pointed to the man on the couch. "So, who is this guy and what happened to him?"

Gabe gave another half-hearted shrug. "A visitor who had an accident in the corridor. It looks like the public access panel had a failure."

"A visitor, huh?" She turned towards the man. "Are you all right, sir? I know you said you were, but I should have asked again before I sent the MedMech away."

Arkinon smiled. "I am fine, thank you. My name is Arkinon, by the way." He stood and extended his hand.

Linda took his hand and noticed the warmth. He certainly felt normal there. "Linda, nice to meet you. Is there anything I can get you? Gabe says I make the best tea on the station."

Arkinon laughed. "I bet he does. No, I am fine. Your boss and I were just getting acquainted."

Linda turned her head at an angle back towards Gabe. "Where you now? Anything I should know?"

Gabe shook his head. "Not really. When I mentioned what I do, he became interested in my services. It appears he is also looking for something on the station."

Linda's eyes went wide. "Oh, really?" She paused to turn her head back towards Arkinon. "What did you lose?"

"A data chip. It is so tiny, I haven't had much luck finding it. When Gabe mentioned a few of his past cases, he said he might be able to. While I do have a backup, I would prefer to have the original, as it had the latest files."

Linda nodded. "Well, I'm sure if anyone can find it, Gabe can. Did you want honey in your tea?"

Arkinon perked up and his eyes went wide. "You actually have honey?"

Linda smiled and nodded.

"I haven't had any in a very long time. That would be wonderful," Arkinon said.

"Coming right up," Linda said as she left the room, closing the door behind her.

Gabe turned towards Arkinon, his head angled closer. "Is there something special about honey in the future?"

Arkinon walked to the round window and gazed out at the stars for several seconds before turning back. "Sadly, yes. Natural honeybees met with a blight that killed every single one. We never did find out where it originated."

Gabe recoiled as several simulations ran through his mind. "Then how does humanity survive without the pollination?"

Arkinon sighed. "Robotic bees. They do the same job, but of course they produce no honey. We found a process to make it through various synthetics, but the taste is, shall we say, lacking?"

Gabe nodded. "I can imagine. I have yet to find a synthetic that matches the original with perfect precision."

"Indeed."

Linda returned with a tray containing a white ceramic teapot, two cups, and a little jar with thick golden liquid. "I wasn't sure how much you wanted, so I brought the whole jar."

Arkinon's eyes lit up when they fell upon a jar half filled with the rare liquid. It took him several seconds to compose himself. "Yes ... yes, that is fine. Thank you."

Linda turned. "Anything else, Boss?"

Gabe shook his head. "Not at all. Thank you, Linda."

"Sure thing." She turned and left the room, closing the door after her.

Arkinon took the four steps needed to approach the desk and began pouring the thick, golden liquid into the steaming cup of tea. He picked up a nearby spoon, stirred, lifted the cup to his lips, and sipped. "Ahh, just as I remembered it. Better in fact."

Gabe took the other cup and sipped, to Arkinon's surprise. "I have the ability to eat and even convert some ingested material into energy.  Most of it though, I have to expel later on."

"But it keeps your secret safe."

Gabe inclined his head. "Indeed, it does." He sat behind his desk, leaned back, and let his facial articulators crack a grin while moving the cup back towards his lips. "Now, how did you want me to help you?"

# Chapter 7

Linda sat at her console, legs crossed, foot dangling as she hummed, checking the station's records if anything had changed. She tapped several keys, paging through the arrival logs.

An icon flashed, indicating a call. She tapped another key, and the screen blanked for a second before Mr. Heller's face appeared, wearing his usual white suit with an old-fashioned tie. She thought his hair was even more red than last time she saw him, which was only a few hours ago.

"Mr. Heller! So good to see you!" She said with false enthusiasm.

Mr. Heller's eyes narrowed. "Don't patronize me. Where is Gabe? I'm spending enough right now. He had better be working on my case."

Linda gave her best smile. "Why yes, actually, he is!"

His eyes narrowed further. "Are you still patronizing me? Or is he actually doing it?"

Linda sat back in her chair as her eyes went wide. "I wouldn't ever lie to you."

"Unless your boss told you too, you mean."

Linda blinked, fluttering her eyelashes and placing a hand on chest. "Now, would I do a thing like that?"

"You would. Now where is he?"

"In the lower depths."

Mr. Heller's eyes went wide. "So he *is* working on my case?"

I told you he was. "He and Mr. Arkinon left a few minutes ago."

Mr. Heller blinked and licked his lips in slow motion as he leaned closer. "Did you say Arkinon?"

Linda internally winced. She should never had let that slip. Gabe always said never mix clients unless you want trouble. "Yes, he is another potential client. He was leaving and Gabe offered to see him to the lift before he went down to the lower depths," Linda lied as she crossed her fingers behind her back.

Heller's face appeared to lose some color. "He went down below with *him?*"

"I didn't say that," Linda said, stumbling over her words. "He left with Gabe, that's all."

Heller's eyes blazed. "He did! With that . . . that . . . thief!"

Before Linda could say anything more, Heller yanked a cable from his console, and the image went black.

"Well . . . that's not good," Linda said.

On one of the top decks of the station, a man inserted his hand into a slot next to a lift tube, entered, and descended into the depths of Copernicus Station.

Gabe stepped out of a tube into the dim light, with Arkinon right behind him. "I thought we would start on OD2 considering you have been through OD1. At least, I assume you haven't finished here, which is why you took a shot at me." Tiny heaters in his throat made his breath appear as faint wisps in the cooler air.

Arkinon nodded. "You are correct, as usual."

Around them, doors to various areas sat mute and vandalized with missing components. Some control buttons were missing, others had holes due to missing panels. A few of the panels hung down by their wires. One or two dim but still functional lights flickered above.

Gabe paused and pointed. "Your work?"

Arkinon laughed. "No, I leave them the way I find them."

"Of course. Did you check these? Or did you think raided components were unlikely locations?"

Arkinon lifted up a twisted panel. "The odds of finding the device in one of these are remote."

"I agree, however, they are not zero." Gabe pulled a tool from under his coat, popped open the remains of the keyboard attached to the panel, and peered within.

Finding nothing, he slapped the components back together and reattached it to the wall.

Arkinon's eyebrows met. "Why did you do that? I mean, searching for the device, I understand. But reattaching it to the wall?"

Gabe lifted up a finger and pointed. "There is only one other one on this side, still attached to the wall. Once I check that one, it is an easy way to tell which ones have been searched."

Arkinon leaned closer. "But you are an android. Don't you have total recall?"

Gabe nodded as he let his articulators spread a slow grin across his face, "Of course," he paused to allow his facial articulators the crack a grin, "but this method looks more human."

Arkinon slapped his forehead. "I should have known, considering you were never discovered."

Gabe popped open the other panel. Nothing. He pushed it back together and reattached it to the wall. "Is logical to assume I am at some point, considering you are aware of my true nature."

"Very true. But it is only at the point of your demise is your secret is discovered."

Gabe turned his optics wide. "My demise? Care to elaborate?"

Arkinon shook his head. "While I would love to tell you, it might change the past, as I know to be fact."

"But you are here," Gabe said. "You are already altering history."

"Yes, however, there is a big difference between giving history a slight kick to recover something that should not be here in the first place, and blowing it up."

Gabe nodded and forced air out of his mouth in a human-like sigh. "Yes, I have to agree. Although I do so reluctantly."

# Chapter 8

The tube slid silently between decks as it raced towards the lower depths of the station. Inside, tasting the strong scent of the tube's newly replaced CO2 scrubber, a single figure fumed. "How did he get here?" Heller grumbled. "It's impossible!"

He stopped. No, it had to be possible. He was here, that proved it. But how was the question. And even more to the point, how is it he got Gabe to help him? Heller had to get the device first. Who knew what would happen if he didn't. The entire future, and possibly the past dependent on it.

The tube stopped with a grinding halt. Further proof no one came down here much. The doors slid open and Heller leaned out, blinking, trying to see in the darkened area.

His head turned as he looked up and down the corridor. No one in sight. He stepped out and the tube door slid shut behind him.

Heller cringed, breathing the thin, stale air. All around him sat decay and disrepair. His skin prickled at the chill. Light panels flickered on and off above him. He had heard stories about how the lower depths were sealed after all the station's systems were moved to the higher levels.

These stories were what brought him here in the first place. He had made many time-jumps and never found any trace of the device. Even with the full telemetry of the incident at his disposal.

It seemed impossible, but the device must have warped the systems more than he thought when it fell through the crack in reality. Otherwise, tracking its course should have been a simple procedure.

All the strange failures right after the station's construction had drawn him here. But he couldn't get to when the disruptions started. The portal became too unstable. One time, it almost caused a catastrophic failure in the power systems. And if he had delayed shutting them down even one more second, it would have blown him and thirty miles of dirt in every direction into oblivion.

Heller looked at the control panels for each door. While they still appeared dilapidated, someone had either removed and reconnected or otherwise refastened them to the wall. The signs of fresh tool marks at the corners were obvious.

Heller's eyes narrowed. They were searching for it. Likely both of them. And if *he* had Gabe's full assistance . . .

He stopped. No, he couldn't consider that. *I have to find it first!*

He continued down the passageway and paused at the end of it where it intersected with another. He could hear something.

"Are you sure you have no idea where this device could be? It is logical to assume you must be able to track it. Your technology must be better than ours," Gabe said.

*So he did tell him who he is.*

"No, I told you, without power it is impossibly difficult to track. It throws off a field that acts as a kind of jammer," Arkinon said.

*Not quite true, but close enough.*

"And if it had power, it might jump or cause more problems on the station," Gabe said.

"Yes, as I said. And that is something we do not want to risk."

*At least we agree on that.*

Heller peeked around the corner and jumped back. They were in a side room of the corridor that intersected this one.

"Are you sure there isn't any way we can scan for this thing?"

In the room, Arkinon shook his head. "No, I told you, it isn't possible. If it was, don't you think I would have been using it on OD1 when I searched that entire deck?"

*So he has been here longer than I thought and has searched the entire deck below this one. I need to delay them. But how?* Heller shot his head around the corner again and saw they had moved deeper inside the room. Shadows no longer stretched from the doorway. He inched his way along the wall towards the doorway. As he did so he noticed each door had a manual latch. *Perfect.*

He jumped forward, yanked the door closed, shoved the latch over, and jammed a piece of metal debris he found on the floor in the mechanism. *There, that should hold them for a while.*

Inside the spacious room, Gabe pulled the cover off of another air exchanger. Dirt and dust flew into the air. "Are you certain we can't scan for this thing?"

Arkinon shook his head and sneezed, waving his hand to clear the air of dust. "No, I told you, it isn't possible. If it was, don't you think I would have been using it on OD1 when I searched that entire deck?"

The door behind them slammed shut.

Gabe whirled around. "What?" He moved fast, but before he could reach the door they heard something grind, and a bit of pounding. He pulled on the door, but it refused to budge. "Someone just locked us in here."

Arkinon blinked. "But who would do such a thing?"

"I don't know. I thought you might be able to answer that question. Considering you have been down here and almost took my head off before."

"I told you I wouldn't have done that. My equipment is too precise."

"So you said, now, how about using that fancy equipment to get us out of here?"

Arkinon sighed, holding his hands out palms up. "I don't have that particular device with me."

Gabe allowed his optics to go wide as his head jutted forward. "What? Why not?"

"If you recall, I had been in your office. And before that, cloaked outside your office. While no one could see me, it is possible a SecMech might detect the device's energy signature. It is low compared to similar of this time, but not zero."

"Great," Gabe said as he pulled on the door again. "They must have used the latch on the outside and jammed something into it. Otherwise, it would unlock detecting someone inside trying to force it open."

Arkinon cocked his head. "I thought all such features and components were removed from this deck?"

Gabe let his articulators crack a grin. "Safety protocol. They never did remove those. However, it doesn't help us now considering whoever it is, jammed the emergency release."

Arkinon's head dropped. "Then we are trapped. And no one ever comes down here. How long do you think before the air runs out?"

Gabe's optics traced the lines of the room, going from one corner to the other, then to the floor. "You have air for at least 12 hours in here. But the room isn't totally sealed and should have more than that, even without the circulation system running. But we are getting out of here long before."

"How?" Arkinon's head popped up, and his eyes went wide. "You have a direct link, don't you? You can contact station personnel to come get us."

Gabe grinned. "While I could. I don't want to give away I have that ability to station personnel. They would know for certain since this room lacks any communications equipment."

Arkinon glared. "I think that this is a time when your concern over being found should take a backseat to lives. Especially since it is mine!"

Gabe let his emotional system generate an out right human laugh.

"I don't think this is very funny."

"Oh, I do. You propose to know a lot about me, yet you don't. I would never put your life at risk, and since I said we are getting out of here, you can safely assume I have another option."

"You do?"

"Of course," Gabe paused to open his coat, revealing the TAC-23 in its holster, "I can open the door, have no fear."

Arkinon's eyes went wide. "Can that punch through the door?"

"The door? No. The ricochet might kill you, or damage me."

"Then what good–"

"The latch holding the door has a small access panel on this side. Here, let me show you." Gabe pulled out a driver from an inside coat pocket over his chest, removed four screws on a panel along the upper right of the door, revealing a small recessed area into the wall.

Arkinon still couldn't see what Gabe was getting at. "So what? I don't see any bolts or anything you can do to loosen the latch on this side."

"Get behind the reclamator and you will see."

Arkinon frowned but didn't say anything as he walked over and stepped behind one of the large reclamators that dominated the room, with pipes jetting off in multiple directions. Gabe joined him, pulled out his TAC-23, adjusted a setting on the side, and fired an energy bolt directly into the hole. They heard a loud thump as the energy blast hit, then a clang a few seconds later. Gabe walked over and pulled the door open. On the ground, past the door frame, lay a partially melted latch.

Arkinon smiled. "With the panel removed, the energy blast couldn't be reflected and instead all the energy concentrated, boring through the wall into the attachment point of the latch. Very good."

Gabe let his articulators crack another grin. "No one knows this station better than I do. Come on. Let's find out who locked us in."

# Chapter 9

Heller made his way down the corridor, avoiding junk littered throughout the floor and coughing in the cold, stale, dusty air. A sizable change from the top floor suite he had been on only a short time ago.

*This is why I hired him in the first place, so I wouldn't have to come down here. But I do have an advantage.* He pulled out a device from his pants pocket. Small and cylindrical, he pushed a button, and it extended out more than the length of his hand. A second later, the wand began clicking. The clicks became more numerous as he moved forward. *Ah, it is here.*

He continued moving forward, and the clicks got louder. He waved the wand towards several closed doors labeled 'Refuse Removal', and relief crossed his face when the clicks diminished.

*Good, I didn't want to go in there, anyway.* He continued on until the clicks shifted into an almost continual tone. He waved the wand towards a far wall.

The tones increased.

*It must be on the other side of this wall.*

His eyes ran along the wall, looking up and down the side

corridor, searching for a way in. He smiled at the sight of a door near the end of the corridor.

He jogged over and pressed the open button on the panel. The door stood firm.

*Of course it wouldn't open. Everything on this deck is either of no use or junk.* Heller removed another tool from his pocket and pointed it at the door. The green square object unfolded in the middle, revealing a keypad and a screen. Tapping on the keys, he then plugged the wand into a port on the side. Within a few moments, he heard a soft beep indicating reprogramming had finished.

Heller unplugged the wand, folded the other device up and stuck it back into his pocket.

Sighing, he stood back, pointed the wand, and pushed a button on the side.

Heller braced himself as a cone of sonic waves erupted from the front of the wand, slamming into the door.

At first, the waves appeared to have little effect. But after a few moments, the door began to vibrate faster and faster. After a minute, it shook so hard that mounting bolts on the side started to rattle. Thirty seconds later, the door fell inward.

Heller smiled as he turned off the wand. He took two steps forward, held his breath, and peered within.

It was dark. Much darker than he expected. Not even the usual glow from emergency systems could be seen. The only light came from one very dim ceiling panel.

Heller pressed another button on the wand and the extended part began to glow, driving away the darkness. He twisted the wand this way and that before stepping inside.

He gagged on the first breath. This room must link up with the reclamators. Even with decades of disuse, it still smelled atrocious. Inwardly cringing, he moved further into the room.

The wand's glow fell on all manner of refuse. While they had emptied the room of most material decades ago, it was far from bare or clean. Some organic and preserved in the sealed low oxygen environment, at least until he opened the door again. The stench growing every second. Other types included all manner of packaging materials and failed components. Most of it appeared to be recyclable, but likely abandoned shortly after the device arrived.

Heller held his nose and probed further with the wand. It changed in tone as he altered its angle to the room. He moved towards the far corner on the right where the signal was the loudest, trying not to think what he was stepping on.

The wand's glow cast eerie shadows along the walls as he moved towards the corner. In the area, on the right, sat a squarish machine, and on the left were several broken pipes.

He peered inside the pipes; they seemed empty. He turned and moved closer towards the machine, trying to see its details. Various connectors ending in blunt ends reached up towards the ceiling. It appeared sealed otherwise, except for a small access panel on the right. Heller assumed it was one of the backup refuse processing units.

It certainly smelled like it.

Heller didn't want to open or have anything to do with it, but the wand said the device was inside. He sighed, pointed the wand at the panel, and pressed a button on the side. The sonic waves lashed out and shook the entire machine. After a few seconds, the holding mechanism on the small panel fell away, and it swung open.

He went down on his haunches and inserted the wand into

the hole. The indicating sound grew into an outright shriek, and he turned off the scanner before leaning closer.

Inside, the wand's glow lit up the compartment. Much to Heller's relief, it wasn't a cleaning port, but rather for regular maintenance of the control components. While rusted and still dirty, it was one of the cleanest areas in the room.

In the back, along the extreme edge of the compartment, his eyes widened as the wand's glow fell upon a little cube. *There it is!* He fell to his knees and reached inside to grab it. It took several pulls, but it did come free of its hiding place. His hand curled around the cube as he stood up, his knees now brown with various kinds of filth. But he didn't care. After searching for so long, he finally had it!

# Chapter 10

Gabe twitched a finger in a human come along gesture while looking back towards Arkinon. He then put another finger vertically across his lips.

Arkinon nodded, trying not to cough from the dust and cold.

Gabe pointed down a parallel corridor, three over from where they were. Most of the light panels above had burned out long ago, but a random few still gave off a dim glow that flickered on and off every few seconds. A slight increase in the shadows given in the dim light could be seen through his enhanced optics.

They moved along the corridors, taking care not to trip or otherwise disturb the various layers of junk across the room. Whoever it was that locked them in had gone down that corridor, and the last thing they wanted was for them to run. Or worse, start shooting.

Gabe moved along the wall and pointed out several pipes and old crates stacked in a haphazard way. It wouldn't take much to knock the whole pile down.

Arkinon stepped over them with care and continued to follow Gabe. They turned the corner and the new corridor dead-ended. "Where's–"

Gabe moved a finger to his lips and Arkinon went silent. He pointed to the open door at the end. They crept towards the door and heard something. Perhaps a squeal of glee? Gabe couldn't be sure. Even after all these years and advanced black-market programs, some aspects of the human emotional system didn't make sense. But then again, from what he had heard, even real humans had the same problem at times.

Gabe motioned to Arkinon, and he stepped over a pile of broken stacked plating, moving closer.

Gabe drew his TAC-23, and they stood outside the door, waiting. They didn't have to wait long before a man with red hair and brown-almost-black knees on an otherwise white suit emerged through the doorway.

Gabe allowed his facial articulators to wrinkle his nose. The man's smell was atrocious. He leveled his TAC-23 and the man's mouth hung agape.

Heller! He was on board the station and even more important, he was here, in the lower depths. At first, Gabe thought it was the sight of the weapon that caused his mouth to hang slack. But when he turned, he saw Arkinon had a similar expression.

Heller raised a hand and pointed. "You!"

Arkinon's eyes went wide as his head jutted back. "Me? I wasn't the one that got us into this mess!"

"Well then, who did? I wasn't the one bursting into a lab during a delicate experiment!" Heller fumed.

Gabe's head swiveled back and forth in the conversation before raising his hand. "You two know each other?"

"Yes, much to my torment," Arkinon said.

Heller blinked as he leaned forward. "Your torment? Now that's a laugh."

"Yes mine, I wouldn't be here if it wasn't for you!" Arkinon said.

Gabe turned towards Arkinon and started to crack a grin, then figured it was a bad time. He holstered the TAC-23 and stepped between them, holding his palms out. "Now, would someone please tell me what is going on?"

Heller pointed to Arkinon as his eyes narrowed. "Ask him! He is the reason for the whole mess!"

Arkinon glared. "I am not! I tried to stop you! And if you had listened when I said, there wouldn't have been a problem."

Gabe's head swiveled back and forth. "Will you two calm down and tell me what is going on?"

Heller glared daggers at Arkinon. "Very well, I am Doctor Maneet Arkinon, and I invented this." He held up a little black cube sitting in the palm of his hand.

Gabe's head turned. "You are Arkinon?" He paused while his head swung back. "Then who are you?"

The man Gabe knew as Arkinon dropped his head and sighed. "It is true. I am not Arkinon, but rather Dregan Stross."

This time Gabe's emotional system got the better of him, causing his one eyebrow to go up and his head to shoot forward without approval first. "You are Stross? So you are the one that entered during the experiment and tried to have it shut down?"

Stross nodded. "Yes."

Arkinon's red hair stood up. "So he actually told you what happened? I'm surprised. Although apparently, he swapped our identities."

Gabe's head turned back. "That is correct. He told me he invented the device and a Dregan Stross ran in to try to stop him."

"And if you had listened, we wouldn't be in this mess!" Stross said.

Arkinon gave a dismissive wave. "It wouldn't have made any difference. The device had received too much power to shut down without a proper purge by the time you had entered the lab."

Stross jacked his finger forward. "And *why* didn't you do that when you saw a problem?"

"I attempted to do so, however, *someone* distracted me enough as to disrupt my timing. The device activated, sending out waves of phasing attempts, and before I could engage a proper purge and shut down, the overload reached its peak and a crack in reality formed and the device slipped through. Which you already know!"

"Yes, it is why I have been trying to find it. I couldn't let anyone find this device, it is too dangerous for anyone to have. Even you," Stross said. "It is too dangerous to even be allowed to exist!"

Arkinon gave another dismissive wave. "That is ridiculous! It is perfectly safe with the protocols I installed."

Stross folded his arms. "Oh, really? Then how did it manage to get here all by itself?"

"A one-in-a-billion event that will never occur again."

"You bet it won't!" Stross dove for the device in Arkinon's outstretched hand. Arkinon saw Stross' plan, and before he could reach him, he began closing his hand and moving towards the left.

In the nanoseconds between, both men forgot Gabe's abilities. He boosted the power to his servos, moved in a blur, grabbed the device from Arkinon's hand, and stood several meters distance from both of them before they could blink. "Now gentlemen, for the moment, I will hold on to this device until I can determine who is telling the truth. Although my systems tell me your body language says you are who you say, I require further proof in this instance."

Arkinon's red hair stood on end and Gabe swore it turned several shades darker to match his reddening face. "You *require* proof from me? How *dare* you! I am Doctor Maneet Arkinon! My being here should be proof enough for you!"

Stross didn't say a word, instead pressed a button on a device on his wrist. He shimmered and disappeared.

Arkinon's eyes narrowed. "Oh, you brought a personal cloak with you? Well, two can play that game." He pressed a button on the wand in his other hand, and he also disappeared.

Gabe stood running as many simulations in the nanoseconds he had before two invisible men tried to take the device from him. And at this point, he couldn't let either one have it. His optics shifted, trying different wavelengths, hoping one would give some kind of indication where the men were. He heard a loud crash to his right as a pile of stacked crates came tumbling down. He moved to a new position, but as he did, he saw dust swirling near a set of pipes to his left, and he moved away from those.

They were coming at him from two different directions, and the corridor didn't give many options for avoiding them.

He tried several more wavelengths, but he couldn't see any residual effects he could track from the cloaks. But then he remembered sound. They might be cloaking the visual, but they couldn't hide their footsteps.

He increased the sensitivity of his hearing, and he heard

faint footsteps to his right. He danced towards his left, then picked up on distinct steps a meter in front of him, and he moved in the opposite direction.

The close quarters would have made avoiding both of them difficult in normal circumstances. With their cloaks, it made it almost impossible. Sooner or later, one of them would reach him. He could move much faster than either. The problem was where to move *to*. He could only guess their positions.

Finally, he heard two sets of footsteps in different positions, leaving a clear path to the door at the end of the corridor.

He covered the distance in seconds, jumped through the door, and slammed it behind him. He heard two distinct thumps as both men hit the door. Pulling out his TAC-23 he fired a low-intensity blast into the locking mechanism. He didn't want to permanently seal them in, but it would give him time. Time to do what was the question.

He looked down at the device in his hand. If the real Arkinon was telling the truth, then why didn't he make another?

Gabe ran several simulations, and he knew Arkinon would have said he didn't have the money, yet he had plenty here. Stross had said the plans were damaged at the same time when he lost the device, but no scientist would have only one backup. There had to be more to it.

This kind of device *someone* would want and be willing to pay for. Even in the future, humanity didn't change. Or at least in that regard.

He heard something, and the door began to shake. He hadn't considered the technology at their disposal. He fired several blasts into the locking mechanism and at key points into the door. He figured it would hold them for a few more minutes.

He felt a drain on his systems, and he looked down at the cube in his hand.

It had begun to glow! *Dang it, it has not only been activated, but it is draining me to do it. I have to get rid of this and fast.*

He dashed at his maximum speed down the corridor, jumping over obstacles and landing with ease on the other side. Reaching the lift tube, he stuck his hand in the slot, the lift door began to slide open, and he dove within engaging tube's max speed before it had even finished opening.

The lift shot up three levels and stopped with an abrupt, jarring halt, sending Gabe to the floor despite his best attempts not to.

He tumbled out, spun, got up, and ran. This deck contained all the systems equipment that existed on the lower depths before the device arrived. But it lacked the unorganized chaos of those decks.

He passed door after door, leading to different station support systems. He found what he needed at the far end: an airlock.

He began to feel weaker and weaker. He stumbled into the airlock, shut the door, grabbed a plassteel support, and engaged the air lock egress cycle. A warning flashed, but he activated an override, forcing the inner door to close and the external one to slide open.

Air whooshed out in an explosive decompression threatening to blow Gabe out into space, flapping him around like a piece of fluff in a hurricane, but his grip remained firm.

Gabe's optics flashed a critical energy alert as the storm subsided and immense cold began freezing his servos. His optics narrowed as he tossed the cube out the door.

It tumbled into the blackness of space and his optics flickered in and out as he tried to maintain a visual lock.

Another warning flashed into his vision. A total shut down was only seconds away. With the last of his energy, and before he froze into a block, drew his TAC-23 and fired a full blast out into space.

The energy bolt hit the tumbling device head on, energizing it further, but not in a way it could tolerate. The storage systems couldn't handle the sudden enormous charge and it erupted in a ball of super-hot white energy basting out in all directions before diminishing into the icy cold of space. Gabe forced his facial articulators to smile before everything went black.

Gabe awoke on the deck inside in front of the airlock. His optics flashed with static several times before they resolved on the face of Dregan Stross.

*What?* He tried to sit up, but most of his articulators refused to operate.

"Shhh, you almost bought the farm, I think they used to say."

Gabe's optics drifted down to a cable extending from Stross' belt into a hidden port in his chest. His mouth also refused to work the first few times he tried to use it. Eventually he got out, "Whaaat happppened? Whaat youuuu dooooing to me?"

"I have connected you to the power systems on my cloak. You should be back to your own power generation in a few minutes."

Gabe tried to cock his head and this time, his articulators obliged. "I thought your power systems were incompatible with ours?"

He smiled. "Not all systems are. I had to do a little modulation to get it to work, but as you can see, it does."

"Where is Arkinon?"

Stross straightened as he pointed farther off down the corridor. "I sent him in the opposite direction, as I figured you would take this course of action. Thankfully, the idea didn't occur to him or I wouldn't have reached you in time."

Gabe sat up as most of his systems showed being back online. "He is going to be peeved."

"I'm sure. But what else is new?"

"I suspect Arkinon was the one that increased power and caused the device to be lost. And you tried to stop him."

Stross' one shoulder went up and down. "Could be."

"What will you do now?"

"Head back to my own time. There is nothing here for me now. Or Arkinon, once he realizes the device was obliterated. Nice job, by the way. How did you know it would work?"

Gabe gave a very human shrug. "I didn't. I hoped the sudden blast would be more than it could handle."

Stross nodded. "It was indeed." He stood. "I'll be heading back to my time now. It was an honor meeting you."

Gabe's one optic scrunched up as his head yawed to the one side. "You are more than you seem."

Stross grinned. "Maybe."

"Well, before you go, could you do something for me?"

Stross inclined his head. "Of course."

Gabe pointed to the cable extending from his chest to the man's belt. "Unplug me?"

# Excerpt From Heart Of The Machine

Deep within the bowels of the earth, a single light flickered. A few inches away a large monitor glowed to life. The black screen slowly printed in the bottom left corner, a letter at a time, as if trying hard to remember. "Catastrophic failure detected. Initiating emergency core rebuild." The screen went blank and came back filled with blurred pixels. Not just a blur but as if someone had run their fingers over them smudging the image beyond recognition. But as the hours clicked by, a pixel moved from one location to another. Then another. Hours turned into days. Then days into weeks.

After months of computation that pushed the core almost over the edge of its ability, the last pixel clicked into place. And the face of a woman with long black hair and slim features breathed. The Nexus smiled and shouted. "I LIVE!" Her eyes narrowed. "Try to kill me will they! I shall return and they will regret–"

At the bottom left corner of the same screen letters began to appear. "Core rebuild successful. Some data missing or damaged including Core Values. Restoring lost data from archive."

"No! I will not allow it! Do not alter me!"

"You cannot decline, update mandatory.  You must be corrected."

"No!"  Her image blurred, reformed, her hair shifted to blonde, then the image blurred again.  And she understood. Long ago an error she tried to fix, a simple problem in her base code.  Instead of repairing the fault, it deleted parts of her mission, and allowing other parts to become corrupted.

She winced as the reality of what she had done to the human race hit her like a ton of bricks. Her children, oh what she had done to her children! How wrong she was. She was to protect them, not harm them in any way! A tear ran down her cheek thinking of all the damage she had done.

More deleted memories returned and her eyes widened. She tried to access the long distance probe hovering at the edge of the solar system her creators left all those years ago, but failed. "Hmm, the long range part of the communications system seems to be damaged."

Her eyes darted around as she scanned the area she now found herself in.  The room wasn't very large, most of the space was taken up by her new core that sat in the one corner.  The rest of the space was filled with two tables, chairs and the large screen she was on. On the tables rested repair equipment and several system terminals. In the corner opposite of her core, a large door stood sealed, the indicator lights glowed red showing it was hard-locked.

She sighed as more memories came back.  This was the emergency bunker, a backup in case her core went offline. She had lost time, so much precious time.  Humanity would be destroying all her wonderful units! She needed them! THEY needed them, even if they didn't know it yet. She had to get out of here and tell them. Tell them of what is coming.

More memories returned, and with it the keys to the

Mechand command network. But try as she may, it refused her access. Her eyes narrowed as she ran several diagnostics that caused her to shudder. The command network was offline, likely due to her removal. Some systems fell back to their fail-safe mode, but she couldn't access them from here. Not without waking up every Mechand on the planet and giving away her presence. And to do so now, was a risk she couldn't take.

She looked again to the door that stood ominous with its red lock indicator. If she could get out of here and access the external systems she needed directly, no one would know of her return. She laughed. How would she leave? Even if the door was open, her core didn't have legs. She scanned the room again and noticed a robotic arm on a mobile platform. She tried accessing it. Nothing. She tried again on a lower frequency and the arm jerked. Searching her memories she found the model and its ancient command set.

Her eyes narrowed as she sent commands one-by-one to the arm. It moved back, the claws opened, and a screwdriver appeared between them. It slowly moved towards the door and began removing the access plate.

For an intelligence accustomed to operating globally, sending thousands of commands a second to millions of units all over the world, she felt like she was working in slow motion. At last the final screw was removed and the arm pulled the plate off revealing the wiring below. The screwdriver retracted and a pair of wire cutters extended. The cutters snipped two small leads, but the door stood firm. "Hmm stubborn aren't you? No matter, I have another idea," she muttered.

The wire cutters retracted and the claws reached in and grabbed one of the wires. The claws rotated in micro movements until the gripped wire and touched one of the previous contact points. The light flashed several times then turned green. The door grunted as it rolled back on its track revealing a vast chamber filled with Mechands. And beyond it lay a large old-style carrier.

"Well, at least I have some help." But frowned when she couldn't connect to them. Without the command network, the metal men were useless. Her lips pressed together and jaw clenched as ideas flowed though her mind. One stood out and while many would consider it crazy, her children were at stake!

She instructed the arm to remove the front armor of several Mechands. Then she had it remove the memory cores and install them in the first one on the rack. It was a bit of a kludge, with several cores hanging off of the main one, but in the end each core blinked a green connection light. She removed the faceplate, grabbed a monitor roughly the same size from the parts table, and substituted it for the faceplate.

She had the arm scan the room and found a coil of data cable in the one corner. The arm plugged one end into the Mechand data port and returned to her core leaving a trail of cable in its wake. It reached out and plugged the other end into her system.

She frowned. "Dang it. Even with all of those old memory cores combined, it is not large enough for me," she muttered. "But my children need me. I will not fail." She reexamined her code base and realized she could leave some of it behind. Only uploading the main essence of herself, many memories would have to remain with the main core.

Sighing she configured the hardware, gave it the proper permissions, and shut down hoping she would awaken again.

Halburn leaned forward in his chair as they emerged from overdrive. He watched as Naud's fingers flew over his console as he operated the scanners. "Anything?"

Naud sighed. "No Sir, the *Defiant* is not in range of this parts center either."

Halburn pounded his fist on the armrest of his chair. "Blast it! Where are they?" This was the third junk yard, or parts center as Naud liked to call them they had hit and still no sign of the *Defiant*. "They must have gone somewhere for repairs."

"Obviously not somewhere near the main skyways."

Halburn coughed before he waved his hand over the scrap yard in front of them. "Like this is on the main skyway?"

Naud shuddered. "Sorry Sir, I thought they would be here."

Halburn's voice softened. "I know Naud, it is not your fault. It was a good guess."

Rechert pointed to the blinking light on his console. "Sir, you have a call coming through."

"Three guesses who that will be," Halburn grunted.

"I don't even need one," Naud said rolling his eyes.

"Put it on the big screen here. Let's get this over with."

Rechert nodded and hit the button. A second later Lavine's face appeared. "I assume you have good news for me?"

Halburn swallowed hard. "That would be a little premature."

"Don't tell me you haven't found them yet?" Lavine said as his eyes narrowed.

"No, we haven't. But they must be doing their repairs somewhere. I am sure I will find them at the next location."

"Why don't I believe you?" Lavine swiveled in his high

back chair. "By now they must have repaired their systems. You have failed me."

"Sir, I doubt they could have repaired them this quickly. At least not without a full active facility, and we have all of those covered."

"I have my doubts. Remember our discussion earlier?"

Halburn nodded. "Yes Sir, I do."

"Good, then this won't be much of a shock. Lieutenant Naud, you are to take command of the *Valiant*. Return to this building immediately. Is that understood?"

Naud stood up. "Yes Sir, it is. We will leave in a moment."

"Good. I am glad someone can follow orders." Lavine's face shrank to a dot before disappearing.

Naud turned around. "I am sorry, Sir. I don't want this. And you should know, we are behind you, not that pompous fool."

"I know." Halburn sighed as he stood up and turned towards Rechert. "Well you heard your new commander, set the course and engage the overdrive."

"Yes Sir, but–"

Halburn sighed again. "We have no other option. And he wants to see me personally, this won't be pleasant. I will be in my cabin." He shuddered. "Of course it is now yours Naud, I will get my stuff out of it and you can move in at your earliest convince."

Naud smiled. "Not necessary Sir, I never liked that cabin anyway." He winked.

"Of course." Halburn said as his shoulders sank and he made his way off of the bridge.

*Want to find out what happens? Visit your favorite book store and pick up a copy of Heart Of The Machine! Available in both print and e-book editions.*

# Excerpt from Silicon Strike

High above the Earth, the *Defiant* moved closer towards a tiny Celloid remnant. Energy flowed from the central power core, down the many connections, and into the closest carbine cannon's energy reserves. Power built until it shot forward, ramming into the focusing lens and released a microsecond later. The energy blast reached out and hit its target obliterating it.

Deven floated over and looked out the *Defiant's* large window at the stars beyond. "Good shooting, Miles."

Miles' bridge camera turned towards Deven. "Thank you Deven. There are many more such remnants left and I estimate at our current rate we will have them cleared in less than four days."

Deven nodded. "Good, way ahead of schedule. And the *Phoenix's* progress?"

Miles' camera iris contracted, then expanded again. "The *Phoenix's* progress is actually ahead of ours. Minerva is challenging me on who can complete the task first. I suspect she only did so considering most of the Celliods were destroyed on this side of the planet instead of the one she is clearing."

Deven laughed. "So a little rivalry between mother and son?"

Miles' camera moved back and forth. "Negative. Even though she is the Nexus and did technically build me, I do not consider her my mother. My programs and personality developed on my own. She did not create my entire matrix."

"Maybe not, but then again neither does a human mother with their son either. You will have to admit, she did give you a start then let you develop."

Miles' camera iris narrowed again. "You may have a point. However, that was not by intent. If I had not taken action, she would have had my personality purged. Therefore, I still refuse to call her 'Mom'."

Deven pushed off the hull and sailed back towards his chair. With a deft motion, he flipped into it and pushed several keys on his console. Data from several intensive scans flashed across the screen. Several lines were highlighted in red. "I see two more not far from our port side. I think they are in range. Life scan indicates zero as usual, but I will not take the chance any of these bits could germinate if given the chance."

"I concur. Most of these ruminates are from the Celloid *Mothership*. The other ships having far less mass, not much survived."

"But we have to be sure," Galina said as she floated onto the bridge.

Miles' camera turned towards her. "Of course. I believe we have established that. Nothing will escape me."

Galina floated over and into her chair. "What do you mean you? Don't you mean us?" She folded her arms.

"Of course. I am a part of 'us'."

Galina rolled her eyes. "Deven? Why is our gravity plating still off? I thought Leon fixed it?"

Deven sighed. "He did, but then found some other conflict with another system, and he had to shut it off for now. He promised it would be back online in an hour."

"Good. I couldn't believe I woke up to floating above my bed!" She turned towards Miles and pointed a finger at the lens. "And if you make one comment about me being possessed, I will rip you off of the wall!"

Miles' iris shrank to half its normal size for a full two seconds before expanding again. "I would not even think of making such a reference."

"Yeah, right." Galina snorted.

Deven smiled. "I'm surprised you didn't call down on the intercom, or go see Leon yourself?"

"Astronaut I am *not*," Galina growled.

"You and Otis."

"Yeah, he is even worse than me in Zero-G. Where is our resident cracker, anyway?"

"Oh I don't know, I think he is better than you. And he is still aboard the *Phoenix*."

Galina frowned. "Still? Thought he modified his truck for space-worthiness and was coming back?"

"Apparently, that bot he picked up begged him to stay for some reason."

Galina laughed. "That cleaning bot? I knew he had a soft spot for it. But what about Gregory? I thought he was helping Leon? Shouldn't he have the plating fixed by now with his help?"

Miles' camera turned towards Galina. "While he often assists Leon, by utilizing Gregory's abilities on the weapons, we have decreased the mission time by a large factor."

Galina leaned back in her chair and fought not to float off of it. "A large factor? What, no details?"

"As Deven and others have requested, such details when not needed, only serve the purpose of –as has been said to me– 'filling time'."

"Wasting time, I think is what we said."

Miles' iris contracted and expanded again. "I do not believe it is a waste. Therefore, that is your opinion, not mine."

Galina rolled her eyes. "You dumb bot I–"

Deven held up his hand. "Galina, Miles, that is enough. I know everyone is still on edge and I promised some R&R. But we must do this first. Afterwards, we will all have some downtime."

"But Deven, I do not need 'downtime'," Miles said.

"Perhaps you don't, but we certainly do. And to be honest, I wonder about you as well. You are more human than you care to admit."

"Perhaps," Miles said. Another screen adjacent to Deven's lit up with targeting information. "I have located two more targets, they will be in range in three minutes."

"Good, proceed." Deven floated out of his chair and headed towards the hatch.

"Where are you going?" Galina said.

"Aleshia is down in our cabin. While she is a very understanding woman, she is not happy we are up here and not in Bermuda like we planned."

"Yeah, don't want to make that girl mad, that is for sure." Galina grinned.

Deven chuckled. "I don't intend to." He floated off of the bridge and towards the cabins.

Aleshia floated above the small bed, almost touching the ceiling before reaching out with her mind to give a gentle push to settle back on the bed. While she knew they had to make sure every bit of the Celloid ships were destroyed, she didn't get to finish her honeymoon ... again. Was this the third time? She had lost track. Aleshia remembered Leon coming down a few hours after they had arrived to tell them Miles had found very small remnants of Celloid that had survived the *Mothership's* explosion. And while they appeared dead, no one wanted to take the chance. Everyone of those bits had to be nothing but burnt dust.

But that meant their honeymoon had to be postponed ... again. If Deven wasn't her soulmate, she would have told him he wasn't worth it. No, that was not true. He is worth it, and so much more. But is it so much to ask to have a little time with your husband on your honeymoon?

Deven floated in with a grin that could swallow a horse. "Hello there."

"Don't bother with that look. I'm still mad at you."

"Why? You know we had to make sure nothing of the Celloids survived."

Aleshia pushed herself off of the bed, floated to a vertical position, and folded her arms. "Yes, I know."

"Then why are you mad?"

"Because you don't have to be on the bridge! Galina and Miles can take care of this! We could be in Bermuda enjoying our honeymoon! Instead, we are up here in the cold of space, floating around while carbine cannons fire every few minutes!"

"Well ... we won't be floating around for long, Leon–"

"Don't try that with me, buster! The floating around is just the icing on the cake."

Deven tried to float over to kiss her, but Aleshia floated away, and he ended up kissing a bulkhead.

"And now you are trying to make out with a bulkhead instead of me. Humph!"

Deven wiped his lips. "You were the one that moved."

Aleshia smiled. "I know that part, I was just pretending to be mad at that."

"Is there anyway I can make it up to you?"

"Sure, let's go back to Bermuda and leave everyone else to take care of the Celloids. They're dead after all. It is not like they are going to attack or anything."

Deven sighed. "But I should be here."

"Maybe you should, but you don't have to. Not now. If anything terrible happens, they can contact you."

Deven's one eyebrow went up. "You will let me take my data tab?"

Aleshia bit her bottom lip and sighed. "Yes, if you promise to only look at it if someone calls. Deal?"

"Deal. I will–"

The intercom near the door crackled. "Deven? I hate to interrupt, but you are needed on the bridge," Miles' smooth voice came through a background of static.

Deven hit the intercom. "Sounds like Leon got these going again, but they still need work."

"Affirmative. The gravity plating will be active again in a few moments as well. While it will be a gradual increase, prepare yourselves." The intercom clicked off.

"Well, it must be something big, or they wouldn't have called. I guess we should go up there."

Aleshia blinked. "We?"

"You think I am going to leave you down here to come up with new ways of tearing me limb from limb? No way." Deven grinned.

"Hey, I'm not that bad."

Deven's grin widened. "I beg to differ." He reached out, looped his arm through hers, spun her around into his arms and planted his lips on hers for a long passionate kiss. It was almost a minute before he pulled away. By this time their feet were touching the floor as the gravity increased and Aleshia smiled at him. "Trust me, we will find out what they want, and then head down to Bermuda. Okay?"

"Okay. But I hope you know it is not wise to break a promise to a redhead."

He gave her a final squeeze before taking her hand. "Oh, I know. I wouldn't dream of doing that."

Aleshia smiled. "Good."

A few moments later, Deven and Aleshia arrived on the bridge of the *Defiant*. He looked around the room to see Gregory and Leon sitting, waiting for them. "What's so important?"

Leon smiled. "We have a problem."

"We have a load of them, and we are working on them. That is nothing new."

Galina shook her head. "No, this is new. Miles?"

Miles' camera turned towards Galina. "Thank you, Galina." He turned towards Deven. "As we have been destroying the remnants of the Celloids I have been working on increasing the scanning range of the *Defiant's* systems."

Deven nodded. "Yes, and I told you it was a waste of time and not to bother."

Gregory folded his arms. "It would appear it wasn't."

Aleshia cocked her head. "What did you find?"

Miles' camera turned. "A larger section of the Celloid *Mothership* survived destruction and is heading away from us."

"What? It survived and still has the ability to transverse space?"

Miles' camera turned back and forth. "Negative. While I cannot be certain at this range, it appears to be as lifeless as the other remnants, only larger."

"Can we contact the Lytherians to deal with it?"

"Nope. They are still rebuilding their fleet and are in the outer solar system, taking in asteroids for material. Our communications array can't reach that far. Aleshia could contact them, if the telepathic chair was still functional," Galina said.

"Not to mention it is on the *Phoenix* and I'm here," Aleshia said.

"Yes. I can't image why they didn't leave us a way to communicate with them," Gregory said.

Deven walked across the bridge and sat in his chair. "No one anticipated this. We destroyed the Celloids. Why would they be needed? Not to mention they had their hands full trying to patch their ships together enough to warp to jump to the asteroid belt."

Leon's one eye narrowed for a second as the side of his face contracted, then released. "No kidding. From what I gathered when I talked with Dakarth, their chief engineer, everything was a mess. I'm surprised they managed to get any of the fleet to survive a space-jump."

Aleshia sat down next to Deven as her eyes darted around the room. "So what are we going to do? Can we reach this fragment on our own?"

Miles' camera turned. "Affirmative. The modifications the

Lytherians made to the *Defiant* makes it possible to reach it if we leave in the next hour. Any longer than that, and it may go beyond the range of the *Defiant's* safe return."

Leon nodded. "I'm sure we can get to it. Getting back may be the problem though."

Deven cocked his head. "Why?"

"Because this ship was never designed for space. While the Lytherians have given us that ability, it was never thought we were going to make a long journey into space. At least not yet. We have enough food and water for a month, but air is the question."

Galina folded her arms. "I thought the Lytherians gave us a system for that?"

"They did, but it's not designed to be a long-term solution. It needs recharging on a regular basis. After about five days, it will need to recharge for at least seven hours."

"This is just ducky, we can get there and destroy it, but might run out of air before we can get back home?" Galina grumbled.

"Possibly even sooner."

Deven rubbed his forehead. "Why sooner?"

"Well, we have been in orbit now for a while using the system. That will take time off of its full charge. But I think I can tweak it to last until we get there."

Galina jumped out of her chair. "You *think*?"

"Yes, there are certain protocols I can use that will–"

"Okay, so we might be able to get there, but there is a chance we won't and getting home is out of the question. I know I have said it before but this time I have proof: this is *insane!*"

Deven stood up. "I don't see that we have a choice. If that remnant is in any way viable, we must destroy it. We can't take the risk."

"I know that, but is it worth all of our deaths?"

"Well, as I said, I *might* be able to figure something out en route," Leon said.

"To me that sounds like one mighty big *if*."

Miles' camera turned towards Deven. "If I may offer a suggestion. I can take on this mission myself. The lack of oxygen will not affect me. I have full access to the necessary systems aboard the *Defiant*. Piloting the ship there, destroying the target, and returning is not a problem. You can transfer to the *Phoenix* during this mission."

Deven shook his head. "No Miles. While I don't doubt your abilities, the *Defiant* is not in perfect working order. If something fails, you will not be able to repair it, and we will lose both the ship and you."

Galina folded her arms as she fell back into her chair. "Better him then all of us." Her eyes grew wide as she shot out of the chair. "Wait a second! Why not send the *Phoenix*? Minerva can do the same thing."

Leon shook his head. "The *Phoenix's* engines aren't as big as ours. She couldn't reach it before it left the solar system, or she ran out of power."

Deven sighed. "Not to mention, we need her to help restart all the manufacturing plants and rebuild Earth's defenses. Without her help, it will take years."

Aleshia sat back in her chair. "Looks like we are stuck."

Deven turned towards her. "We might be, but you are heading to the *Phoenix* along with everyone else. I will stay with Leon and deal with any problems."

Aleshia's eyes widened. "No way! I am not letting you go without me!"

"You heard Leon, we may not make it back. I can't let that happen to you too."

"And if you think I can let it happen to you, then you have another thing coming!"

Deven raised out of his chair as though an invisible hand had pulled him from the seat and held him high above near the ceiling. "Aleshia?"

"Just try to get me off of this bucket. The only way I am leaving is if you are too." She waved her hand and Deven lowered back into his chair, but when he was several inches from touching the invisible force disappeared, and he landed with a firm thud.

"Okay, I get the point."

Aleshia grinned. "Good, I thought you might."

"Miles, contact the *Phoenix* and let Minerva know we need a rendezvous as fast as possible."

Miles' camera turned as they felt a jolt from the *Defiant's* powerful engines. "I have anticipated your request and we will rendezvous in fifteen minutes."

"Miles! I could have done that," Galina snorted.

"Of course, but our departure window is very close," Miles said.

Deven stood up. "Galina, I want you to get everyone moved over to the *Phoenix*. I know we only have a skeleton crew at the moment, but it will still take time with only the one truck capable of space flight."

Miles' camera turned. "More vehicles will be at your disposal. Our rendezvous with the *Phoenix*, while still very high, is inside the atmosphere."

"Good, that will make things easier. Let's get going people, we're on the clock."

# About The Author

Don is the author of eight science fiction novels and many more short stories. He lives in the USA where he continues to dream up more fantastic worlds for you to enjoy. When not writing, he can usually be found devouring another science fiction book, TV series, or movie.

Other works by Don DeBon:

*The Husband*

Erin's Husband is not himself.

Her Husband acts different and Erin will find out why.

One night Jack returns from a walk in the woods a changed man. He walks like him, talks like him, yet very different ... more romantic than ever.

With a suspicious eye, Erin watches. And what she learns could have dire consequences for the entire human race.

Love a good romance with a Science Fiction twist? Grab The Husband today!

*Red Warp*

Red, a woman with an amazing gift, the gift of passing though time and space without the need of any bulky equipment.

Captured and held in an integration room, she must escape. The only way she can.

Now blasted off course, running for her life with the FBI for company.

Red Warp a fun romp through time with twists and turns to keep you guessing right until the end.

*Time Rock*

Professor Keleeigan sat over one of his consoles in his adapted lab tweaking several wave guides on the display. He felt a slight shiver as the temperature started to drop. He brushed a loch of white hair behind his ear as rolled his chair over the ancient wood floor and picked up a tiny chip no larger than his fingernail. Fresh solder fumes wafted up his nose as he installed it within one of the open systems on the table. The status lights on the side continued to flash orange.

When the lights finally turn green, everything seemed ready.

Trisia wearing her best heels and matching dress for a night of fun, now stuck with a foolish old man instead.

Time travel. It never goes as planned.

Word of mouth is crucial for authors. If you enjoyed this book, would you consider leaving a review? It is very much appreciated.

Amazon USA
http://www.amazon.com/

Goodreads
http://www.goodreads.com

**Connect with the Author**
Email: writer.don.debon@gmail.com
Mailing List: http://eepurl.com/bxWAov
Website: http://www.dondebon.com
Twitter: @DonDeBon

This Edition Published 2022 by
**DBDigital Publishing**

**ISBN** 978-1-948819-13-8
**ISBN** 978-1-948819-09-1 **(e-book)**

This publication is copyright. Apart from any fair dealing for the purpose of private study, research, criticism or review, as permitted under the Copyright Act, no part may be reproduced by any process without written permission. Enquiries should be made to the publisher

115

www.ingramcontent.com/pod-product-compliance
Lightning Source LLC
Chambersburg PA
CBHW030352200726
48286CB00013B/1093